Addiction

Chapter 1

"So, Doc, ahh crazy question - is it possible to be um, like, addicted to a person?" It was a crazy question and Tom was somewhat embarrassed by even asking it, but it was a question that he had been wondering about for days now.

The doctor, actually a psychologist, was a bespectacled balding man in his fifties, who had heard a whole lot of crazier things in his twenty odd years of practice. He was aware that Tom was serious, and he needed more information before he could give an answer. "Do you think that you are addicted to a person Mr. Jensen?"

Tom took a deep breath and scratched his forehead before answering "Well, there's this girl that I kinda like, I guess, but I like lots of girls if you know what I mean." He glanced up at the doctor who was writing something on his clipboard, then continued. "I mean, I kinda play the field right now, you know, I'm not really ready to settle down just yet. But then there's this girl who is hot, and I went out with her a few times, and it was good you know, but it was just like any other time and any other girl. She was just a… a distraction, I guess. You know she was fun and all, but not any more than that." He stopped to think about what else to say because the rest was tricky.

The doctor looked up and adjusted his glasses "Go on Mr. Jensen, you're doing fine."

Another sigh and then "Well, we went out like, maybe three times and I was still seeing other girls. She knew that too. I told her that I wasn't exclusive with her from the beginning, it wasn't like I was hiding it you know. And then, one night, she calls me out of the blue and says she wants to see me. Actually, she told me that she wanted sex. It wasn't the first time we had sex either. So, I went over and, like one thing leads to another you know, and we get undressed and she, like pulls my face down to her… you know."

"She wanted you to perform oral sex on her." the good doctor finished for him.

"Yeah that's it. So, like I go down there, and I smell her… and it's like there's something about her smell. It's not normal, but not in a bad way or anything. It was like I couldn't get enough of her smell, and she kept encouraging me to. 'Keep smelling me' she says and 'that's it, breathe it all in'. It's like she knew something, but at the time I didn't realize anything was wrong. I just kept smelling her scent and it was like heaven." He glanced up at the doctor and realized that he was listening intently this time, not writing anymore.

"Can you describe what you felt as you were smelling her?"

"I really didn't think so at the time but later when I thought about it, I realized that I felt… almost high. Like I was intoxicated by her odor. The weirdest part of this is that I keep having these cravings now. I can't stay away from her for more than a day, or I have… withdrawals."

The doctor adjusted himself in his chair, as if he had become uncomfortable, and asked his next question. "Can you explain what you mean by 'withdrawals'?"

"Well, I haven't gotten sick or anything, but I get really tense and I can't think clearly. All I can think about is getting back between her legs and smelling her and licking her. Even when I'm with another woman, we could be having sex and I could be eating her pussy" he paused when he realized how crudely he just spoke and looked to see if he had offended the doctor. There was no discernible difference in his demeanour so Tom continued "Sorry, I could be performing oral sex and I'm still thinking about how quickly I can get out of there to go see Ka- the other girl. It's bizarre."

"What about your job, has that suffered at all?" The doctor inquired.

Another deep breath from Tom and then "Yeah, I think about her at work all the time. My boss has noticed that I haven't been myself and was asking me what was going on. I told him that I have some personal issues that I'm dealing with. Doc, it's affecting every aspect of my life lately. If I go more than one day without seeing her, without smelling her, I can't sleep, I can't function, and I'm afraid that it's getting worse."

"When was the last time you were with her?"

"I went to her place last night around eight o'clock and every night I feel the need to go over earlier. Just a few days ago I could hold out until ten P.M. And when I go to her place, even when I just pop in without calling, she's expecting me, like she knows I'm going to show up."

The good doctor sat for about twenty seconds thinking about what he had been told then gave his perspective "Well, to be honest Mr. Jensen, you can't become addicted to a person's smell; however, the juices that an aroused female produces from her vagina can be quite an aphrodisiac to a heterosexual man, and may create the feelings that are similar in fashion to an addiction. It seems to me though that your reaction is much more intense than normal. It has affected all aspects of your life and that is not a good thing. Not to belittle you Mr. Jensen, but I believe that what you are experiencing is all in your head. Perhaps your feelings for this young lady are deeper than what you are willing to admit. Love works in strange ways you know."

"I'm NOT in love with her, if that's what you think. She's cute and all, but she's not really my type."

"But you've slept with her."

"Yeah, she was a good time and all, but I don't want to marry her or anything."

Nodding his head, the doctor of psychology stood up and glanced at the clock on the wall. "I'm going to teach you some exercises to help calm you and focus you. I believe that this will be an easy fix, but you just need to focus your brain on something other than the young lady that has got you in such a fix. I'm also going to recommend that you get an over the counter sleep aid to help you get a good night's rest. I think you can take care of this relatively easy Mr. Jensen, and you'll realize that you are not really addicted to her at all, just infatuated."

"I hope you are right doc."

Chapter 2

Later that evening, Tom started feeling the urge again around five P.M., and he immediately started doing the breathing exercises that he had learned earlier. Deep breathing and shaking out the stress helped him feel better after ten minutes and he was confident that it was going to work. The doctor told him that if he could resist going back to her, his body would forget the craving and he could go back to his normal life. It lasted about twenty minutes while he attempted to keep himself busy, but then he started to think about her again. He resisted for ten minutes then did the breathing again until he was relaxed and thinking clearly again. This time it took him twenty minutes to calm down and it was now six o'clock.

He made himself busy cooking dinner and tried singing along to the radio, but soon found himself with the cravings again. He glanced at the clock and was surprised to see that it was only ten past six and he felt even more jittery than before he did the calming exercises the second time. He had planned to tough it out until eight o'clock and then take a sleeping pill, hoping that if he made it through the night, he would put as much distance between himself and her as possible.

He tried to ignore the feelings that were building in him, he was still cooking after all, but soon he was so preoccupied that he wound up burning his meal. Hungry and angry at himself, he sat down and started once more with the breathing. Even doing his exercises, he still couldn't calm his incessant cravings and after just ten minutes of trying, he decided he needed the sleeping pills. The problem was that when he left the doctor's office, he had forgotten to stop at the pharmacy and that meant that he had to go out now. Grabbing his keys, he headed out the door.

He nearly made it to the pharmacy before he turned and headed toward Kayla's house. He was convinced that she had done something to him, and he was determined to confront her and find out what. He broke more than one speed limit on the way and finally pulled into her driveway. It was seven o'clock.

Tom jogged up the front steps and stopped at the door. He took a deep breath and let it out between pursed lips and then knocked loudly. As he waited rather impatiently, he noticed that his usually steady hand was trembling badly. He made a fist and crossed his arms over his chest. A few seconds later, he heard a female voice from inside the house call out "You can come in Tom." It was definitely Kayla, but how did she know it was him?

He opened the door and walked into the foyer, closing the door behind him. He made his way down the short hallway to the room he assumed she would be, and as he walked, he was struggling with conflicting emotions. On one hand, he was angry with himself for being so weak and angry with Kayla because he was sure that she had something to do with his problem; on the other hand, he was excited and couldn't wait to be in the same room with her.

He turned right and walked into the living room and was relieved to see she was lounging on the couch. She looked the same as always, shoulder length, fiery red curly hair, a smattering of freckles on her cheeks and forehead, thick, soft red lips, and a cute little nose. Her eyes were what Tom always noticed first though. Her eyes just had a way about them that he found super sexy. No matter what the conversation was about or what she was looking at, he thought that her eyes were her best feature. Her body wasn't too shabby either, although in his mind, she could have lost a few pounds. She wasn't fat by any means, but she had a little more belly fat than he preferred. He also thought that her ass had too much cushion. Even though he would agree that she was a beautiful woman, and perfect for some lucky guy, she wasn't right for him because he wanted to be seen with a Barbie doll girl.

"Hi Tom, I've been waiting for you." She said, smiling sweetly.

Tom was confused because he hadn't told her he was coming over. "Why, were expecting me?" he asked.

"Come on Tom, we both know that you can't resist me."

Tom had all he could do to keep himself from rushing over to her and diving between her legs, but his anger was also rising. "WHAT THE HELL DID YOU DO TO ME!?!" he shouted, stepping around a table, but resisting the urge to jump on her.

Showing no fear, Kayla said "Sit down Tom."

Feeling a drop of sweat rolling down his temple Tom was shocked by her attitude. After all, he was a strong man, and she was a just a woman. He could easily have his way with her if he wanted, and yet she didn't seem the least bit worried. He fought the urge to keep yelling and said, "I don't want to sit down, I want to know the truth."

"Tom, when I tell you to do something, I expect you to do it and not question it. Now sit your ass down."

He paused for only a second, and then he sat on the footstool in front of her. If someone had asked him later why he had sat when she ordered him, he would have said it was because he wanted to know what she had done to him, but the truth was, he didn't know why he obeyed her.

"Good boy." She beamed brightly again. "Okay, so you want the truth huh? I knew that you would soon enough. So, where to begin? Well to start with, the company I work for, Scent Designs, started testing what we like to call 'designer scents'. The idea is that they will take a sample of a clients DNA and use that to make a scent that is perfectly matched to that person. They needed a variety of DNA from several different people, and I volunteered. They made scents for twenty different people and started testing it on the first five volunteers. I was in the last five, so I originally didn't get any of my special scent.

The tests were a success, at first. The first five volunteers were told to bring in their favorite perfume or cologne. They used the store-bought stuff on one arm and the specialized scent on the other. A panel of judges were assigned the task of smelling each arm individually, and then picking which scent they preferred. Apparently, it became quite obvious that something was different when the judges were smelling the designer scents. They all picked the DNA enhanced versions without first being told which arm was which."

"A day after the initial tests were conducted, both the judges and the subjects all started to experience some peculiar side effects. The judges were desperate to get back to the person that they originally smelled. They had become addicted, because of one smell. Meanwhile, the test subjects all begged for more of the scent. Well, the testing should have stopped right then, but instead, the judges and the test subjects were given what they wanted. Each test subject was given more of their individual scent, and each judge was allowed to smell them. I was lucky enough to be able to watch what was happening, and I've got to tell you Tom, I was enthralled."

"These people were relative strangers, but it was as if they had lost their inhibitions. No one got naked or anything, but I'm talking, judges were sticking their noses in places that they would never had done had it not been for the scent, and no of them seemed to care in the least, as long as they got what they wanted. Well after that, all production of new designer scent was halted until our scientists could figure out the whole addiction thing, and the other fifteen test subject were put on hold, no one else could use the stuff. I mean, we wanted something that people were going to love, but not become addicted to."

"Meanwhile, the original five test subjects and judges continued on with the experiment. At least for a few more days anyway. You see, one other side effect became apparent after a few days of usage. Parts of the test subjects bodies were...enlarging and becoming more sensitive with each application of the scent. It was determined at that point that there were too many risks to continue the program, so it was shut down. All the people who became addicted had to go through specialized detox. There was no long-term damage done, but the rest of the designer scents that were made were all supposed to be destroyed. I didn't want my batch to be destroyed Tom, I wanted what the test subjects had, and I needed to find a way to get my scent before it was destroyed."

"Luckily for me though, the guy that was responsible for destroying the samples likes me. He's a nice guy, but he's kind of a geek, not at all like you. All I had to do was bat my eyelashes a few times and promise him a blowjob and he snuck out my sample. Then I just needed to pick the perfect person to be my bitch, and after I found out how good you are in the sack, all I had to do was invite you over for sex and spray on some of my special scent. You were hooked immediately, and every time that you smelled my pussy after that you were more addicted until now."

Tom was incensed and yet he could only think of getting his fix. He started mumbling out loud, his mind a jumbled mess "I knew it was something. I told him but he didn't believe me. He will now though, he has to believe me." Tom didn't even realize that he was talking out loud.

Kayla heard it all and quickly leaned forward "Who did you tell Tom?" she asked. She watched his eyes darting around and realized that he needed a fix to clear his mind. She hadn't yet sprayed herself with the scent so she said "Tom, wait here, I need to freshen up and then you can have this." She pointed to her crotch and saw his eyes light up. "I'll be right back" she assured and quickly hurried to the bathroom. She could hear Tom still mumbling as she went. Once in the bathroom, she yanked her shorts down and grabbed the spray bottle. She pointed the sprayer at her pussy but stopped before she sprayed. A wicked smile played over her face as an evil idea came to her. She bent forward at the waist and with her right hand she pulled her right ass cheek open. Then, with the bottle in her left hand, she placed the nozzle right up against her puckered asshole and squeezed the trigger. She felt the cool liquid spray in her anus and laughed out loud. She felt so wicked and couldn't wait to see Tom's face.

Chapter 3

She walked back to the living room naked and saw Tom perk up when he saw her. She moved to the couch and sat in the centre, spreading her legs wide apart. Tom nearly dove face first into her pussy and started sniffing all around. She watched him with amusement as he searched all around her sex but still wasn't getting what he desperately needed. Finally, he looked up at her in confusion. She burst out laughing at the expression on his face, she couldn't help herself, he looked so pathetic. She took his face in her hands and pulled him up close to her face. "Honey," she cooed "I've got a special treat for you tonight. I've hidden what you need somewhere on my body and it's up to you to find it, if you really want it."

Of course he really wanted it, and he was determined to find it too. Like a hound dog searching for a fox, he started sniffing all over her body, his nose tickling her. He was absolutely frantic as he sniffed up one side and down the other. He went up and down both arms and legs. Her feet had an unpleasant cheesy smell, but he worked his way around every inch and up the back of her legs. Finally, he looked at her and said, "It's not here, I've gone over every inch of you."

Smiling again Kayla said, "You haven't smelled every inch yet." and she motioned to the one part that he hadn't smelled, the part she was sitting on. Her ass. He looked down at where she was sitting and back at her eyes. A tear rolled down his face as he realized how low he was at this point. Kayla reached up and wiped away the tear then said, "If you want your fix, you need to lay on the floor."

A once strong man who would never have let a woman treat him like this a few weeks ago, Tom hung his head dejectedly and rolled onto the floor. His brain didn't want this and kept yelling at him to fight this feeling, but his body craved it so bad that his brain was overruled. He watched as she crawled on top of him and scooted her ass up to his chin. Looking down into his eyes she said, "I'm afraid that you're going to have to go digging for it."

He wondered what she meant as she slid over him. He looked up at her ass and from this perspective it seemed enormous. He started sniffing all over the globes of her cheeks first as she hovered about an inch over him. When that didn't bring the results he craved, he stuck his nose into her sweaty crack and inhaled her womanly scent. Her smell was strong musk but not too unpleasant and he did get just a slight rush as a tiny bit of the designer scent was also inhaled. A little more investigation and he came to the realization that it was not on her ass but in her ass. He whimpered at the thought of what he had to do. He reached up and grabbed her by the waist and guided her asshole to his nose.

"Oh, there you go, you got it now." Kayla said as she let him pull her where he needed. She felt his nose sink into her crack and push up against her anus. She was absolutely loving the feeling of power she was feeling right now and thinking to herself that if it felt this good with one man, how great would it be to have more.

This wasn't the first time Tom had been this close to a woman's asshole, but this was quite different. In the previous instances, he had been the aggressor. Hell, he was always the aggressor with women. In his mind that was the way it was supposed to be. The stronger male was the dominant one while the weaker female was the submissive. What was happening here was all wrong.

He kept sniffing deeply and was getting some of what he needed, but not nearly enough. It was like an alcoholic who only has one wine cooler. It is alcohol, but not enough. As degrading as it was, he was trying to insert his nose into her asshole, but it just wasn't working. Then he heard her say something that made him wince. "Try sticking your tongue up there, that should work." He cringed but he knew she was right. It was a horrible sinking feeling to think that he had to stick his tongue in her ass to get what he wanted, but his craving was so strong at this point that he tried. He tried but her sphincter muscle was too tight. He could feel himself getting frantic until he heard Kayla's calming voice say, "Lick around it gently and it will open for you."

He would try anything at this point, so he started licking all around her puckered anus, lubing it up with his saliva. Kayla enjoyed the feeling of having her asshole licked and this being her first time, she decided then and there that she wanted to do it more. For about a minute that seemed like a lifetime to Tom, he licked her wrinkled brown hole. He was starting to think that licking gently wasn't working when he realized that his tongue was actually sinking in deeper each time, he slid it over. It was loosening so he took a chance and pushed hard and was rewarded as he sank in deeply. He heard Kayla moan loudly, but to him she seemed miles away.

There was a slight tingling sensation on his tongue, and he felt a rush go through his body. It was so intense that his penis expanded rapidly, and his mind came into clear focus. He had definitely hit the pay dirt that he was searching for, and he wanted more. The smell and taste were forgotten as was the depressing feelings he had felt and the shame. What he felt now was his need being taken care of. It was like a vampire who was feeding on the neck of a victim and getting strength from that feeding.

The feelings Kayla was experiencing was quite different. She was shocked at how good this ass play felt and she started rubbing her sopping pussy. She couldn't remember the last time her pussy got this wet without anyone touching it. In fact, she was so turned on, she could smell her arousal stronger than ever before. Even that heightened her excitement. As the feelings intensified, she rubbed her clitoris faster and soon forgot that there was a man beneath her ass.

She lowered herself down, so she was sitting full weight on his face. Her breathing had become a series of short sharp breaths sounding almost like a locomotive chugging down the tracks. "WHOO WHOO WHOO WHOO" Her fingers became a blur, and she stretched her legs out straight which put more weight on Tom's abused face. The muscles in her legs tightened up as the pressure built, this caused her ass cheeks to squeeze together, clamping down forcefully on his nose.

When Tom started getting what he needed out of Kayla's ass he was in heaven, but as she lost control of her muscles and dropped on his face, he was just in pain. At first, the weight of her pressing on his face was bad enough, but at least her chunky ass was soft. He still had his tongue deep inside her and for the moment he was still able to breathe with some difficulty. But when her muscles clamped down, the softness disappeared and became hard. He couldn't breathe anymore, and his nose felt like it was about to snap like a twig. He pushed with his hands, trying to lift her up to relieve the pressure, but in his position, he had no leverage, and the little that he moved her only made things worse when he dropped her. He heard a snap and saw bright lights flash as the pain exploded in his head. He dug his fingernails into her thighs, shaking in agony and yelping, certain that his nose was busted now.

With absolutely no care in the world for the whimpering man underneath her, Kayla started bouncing her butt ever so slightly up and down as her orgasm overtook her. Her body was covered in a sheen of sweat, her muscles ridged, her breath caught in her throat, and her pussy and ass contracting in ripples as she rode the pleasure wave. Sometime during her orgasm, her pussy squirted a small jet of clear fluid which dripped down into Tom's hair, and she lost control and farted. She wasn't screaming during her intense cum, she wasn't much of a screamer anyway; instead, she was gritting her teeth, her eyes rolled back, and her body trembled like a leaf in the breeze.

The agony for Tom intensified when she started to cum because she bounced up and down. Her ass that had been so soft earlier was now hard and unforgiving. Yet throughout the pain, he was still trying to get to the sweet nectar that was slowly dripping out of her ass. His need was being satisfied, his addiction being sated in spite of his pain and his asphyxiation. When she started cumming though, his tongue was forced out by her sphincter clamping down hard. He was just a seat now, for he was not helping her cum anymore. He felt wetness on his head and almost instantaneously his cheeks were filled with a powerful blast of hot fetid air. The gas that escaped her ass was sealed in completely by his face and much of was inhaled in his injured nose. Now his nose felt like it was on fire from the inside, and he started slapping on her thighs with his hands, desperate to dislodge her.

The slapping on her thighs was a minor annoyance after the monumental orgasm left Kayla in a haze of bliss. She sat for another thirty seconds while her heart slowed, and her muscles stopped trembling. Finally, she slid her ass back to his chest, and gasped when she saw his face. He had been completely out of air for well over a minute and had nearly passed out. His face had gone past red and was nearly blue. A pulsating vein stood out on his forehead. His eyes were bloodshot and haggard looking. He had two black eyes and his nose was crooked. There was milky white cream mixed with brownish slime all over his face like a glazed donut. He looked as if he had just fought a heavyweight boxer. His eyes were open and he still awake, but barely. Kayla slapped him lightly on his cheeks until he woke up fully, then climbed off him to let him recuperate.

Tom rolled on his side and held his face in his hands. "You broke my fucking nose." he said, although it sounded more like "You bwoke my fuckin dose." Kayla genuinely felt bad for breaking his nose, but she didn't want him to know that, so she bit her lip and said "Oh you poor baby, you're lucky I didn't smother you to death. Now, if you want to be able to get what you need easier next time, you'll tell me who you talked to about me."

Tom turned back to look at her "What?" he asked, forgetting that he had said anything.

"After I told you about the designer scents you said, 'I told him, but he didn't believe me.'
So who did you tell Tom?"

Tom closed his eyes as he was suffering through the worst headache ever. "I was talking to my psychologist Dr. Hewes, but I ah, I didn't tell him your name, I think. He didn't believe me anyway. Wait till I tell him this story though. Maybe he'll HUUAAAH…" he didn't get to finish his sentence because she suddenly turned and plopped her ass back down on him, this time landing right on his belly. He wasn't expecting it and she knocked his breath right out of him.

"You won't tell him anymore because the next time you go see him, I'm going with you."

Confusion would have been evident on Tom's face if his face hadn't been broken and battered. For now, though, he was in too much pain, and he just nodded in agreement.

Chapter 4

Tom spent the night with Kayla, but not in her bed. She made him sleep at the foot of her bed on the floor and she gave him a bag of frozen peas to put on his swollen face. The next morning, he made two phone calls. The first was to his job, which he lied and said that he was much too sick to work and would be out the rest of the week. It was Thursday anyway so he would miss only two days and he had several sick days already built up.

The second call was to Dr. Hewes office. He called before they opened for patients and asked the receptionist if he could get an emergency appointment with the doctor. He told her that he really needed the latest possible appointment, preferably the very last of the day. She told him that he was in luck and could see the doctor at four o'clock that afternoon, the last appointment. He had no idea why Kayla wanted to see Dr. Hewes or why she wanted to be the last appointment, but he really didn't care either. As long as she took care of his needs.

Afterward, he went into the bathroom and looked at his battered face. His nose looked somewhat straighter after he had tried snapping it back into place the night before. He had taken three aspirin and had numbed it somewhat with the frozen peas before trying to re-align it. His face still looked like he had been in a car accident though. His still had two black eyes and his nose was also discolored.

They had breakfast together and Tom asked Kayla just what she had in mind at Dr. Hewes. She grinned a somewhat evil looking grin and said "I think Dr' Hewes will be very interested to find out that you were telling the truth. I was under the impression that doctors were supposed to listen to their patients and try to help them, not dismiss their problems as something in their heads."

"So you're going to tell him about this magical spray stuff then?"

"I'm going to do better than that Tom. I'm going to make him smell it, and you are going to help me. That is if you want more of my pussy." Tom knew that she wasn't just talking about her pussy, but about the spray that he would be having withdrawal symptoms from if he didn't get his daily fix in time. The thought of having someone else addicted to Kayla made him nervous. What if she ran out of the spray? She did say after all that it wasn't being made anymore. Plus, he was a little bit jealous.

"I don't think I'm okay with helping you do that." He said, "I mean, why would you even want to do that?"

Kayla put her fork down, picked up her napkin and wiped her mouth before looking him in the eyes. "First of all," she said coldly "you don't get to have an opinion. You're just an ass eating slave. Second, if you don't like it then you can leave anytime, I'm sure that you can overcome your addiction to me eventually." she picked her fork back up and took another bite of egg before saying while chewing "Why don't you get under the table and put your fucking tongue to work. I'm horny."

Tom sat for a moment looking down at his half-eaten breakfast. He was still hungry, and he was ashamed for having so little willpower. He wanted to tell her to go get fucked but he knew that he wouldn't. he glanced back at Kayla who had resumed eating and then he slid forward out of the chair and onto his knees under the table. It was a small round table with four chairs around it and a white tablecloth covering it.

Once under the table, he felt like he was in a cocoon. He reached over and pulled apart the sides of her robe, exposing her cotton panties. He could faintly smell her womanly odour. Taking both sides of her panties, he edged them down past her thick thighs, around her folded knees and down her calves until they fell off her feet. As he glanced back up at her exposed vagina, he smelled her aroma again, now much sharper than before.

Realizing that he would have difficulty reaching her like she was sitting, she scooted her ass forward to the edge of the chair and sighed deeply as she felt his mouth attach to her moistening pussy. She hadn't sprayed any of the scent on this morning so she knew that he wouldn't get anything out of this other than maybe an erection. For the first few minutes she kept eating her breakfast while he was eating her, but as the feelings intensified, she put down her fork and gripped the side of the table. His tongue was fluttering all around her clit and then he would slide down lower and stick his tongue into her pussy hole before going back to her sensitive clit again.

Something was strange though and Tom realized it the more he licked and sucked her. Her clitoris seemed to be bigger than he remembered it being. He understood that the clitoris was like a miniature penis and that it filled with blood, thereby making it larger, when it was excited, but he had been down here before a few times and he never remembered it being this big. In fact, the first few times he had gone down on her, he had had trouble finding her clit. Now, her clit stuck out more than a half inch and was swelled up to the size of his thumb. It was certainly much more convenient this way and he wrapped his lips around it and whipped his tongue over it as fast as he could.

The sensations for Kayla were inexplicably heightened. To her it felt like he was doing something different than he had done before and it felt divine. She was getting closer and closer and then "AAAAAAAAAAHHHHHHHHHHSSSSSHHHHHIIIIIITTTTTT" she screamed in ecstasy and was overtaken by her orgasm. Her legs clamped together on Tom's head reminding him that he still had a headache, and she felt the sudden urge to pee, although she hadn't had to pee before. She made a split-second decision and decided to let it spray, not sure if it was urine or not. She pushed like she was peeing and felt a jet of fluid spray from her twitching cunt. It only intensified the already overwhelming feelings, and she opened her mouth and screamed again. This time "OOOOOOOHHHHHHHYYYYYYYYEEEEEEEEESSSSSSSSSS". She couldn't remember ever having an orgasm so powerful, or one that lasted so long. It seemed to go on and on and by the time it wound down, she was out of breath, covered in a sheen of sweat, and shaking uncontrollably.

Meanwhile, Tom's face was wedged between her thighs and he was trying not to drown in her ejaculate. He hadn't been expecting the sudden forceful spray and his mouth was filled quickly. Some went down his throat and made him cough. He pulled back and bumped his tender nose causing him to yell in pain and lose his erection.

Once finished, Kayla pushed away from the table and made her way to the bathroom without acknowledging the man kneeling under the table. She walked to the bathroom with a purpose, and it wasn't to clean up or to use the toilet, it was to spray her pussy with another squirt of the designer spray. She didn't know why she did it because Tom wasn't asking for it yet. For some reason she just felt like she needed it. She had noticed after about the third time she had sprayed herself that it gave her a pleasant tingly feeling and calmed her each time she sprayed herself. She didn't know what it meant and right now she didn't care. After she sprayed herself, she lifted the bottle and saw that it was about half empty. For some reason that made her feel nervous about running out and she started to form a plan to ensure that she wouldn't run out.

Chapter 5

They both showered and got dressed and Kayla grabbed the bottle and dropped it in her purse. She was going to leave Tom at her place but then decided he could come with her. She had to go to her job in order to secure some more scent. Ten minutes later they pulled into the three-quarter full parking lot of Scent Designs. Kayla told Tom to wait in the car and went into the building. She didn't bother to punch in because she wasn't planning on working today. Instead, she headed for the laboratory and the one person who could make more of what she needed.

There was at least a dozen people in the lab and the one person that she was looking for was Arnold Peters, the man that she convinced to sneak out her special scent. Arnold was an overweight, balding man with thick glasses and a pimply face. Not the most handsome man for sure and that was why he was so easy to manipulate. She had promised him to suck his dick if he would get her the scent and she hadn't yet paid him. To be fair, she hadn't planned to pay him when she made the deal. She knew that he wouldn't tell anyone because it would mean not only losing his job, but also prosecution. Now however, she needed something else, and she had no choice.

She found him sitting at his chair looking into a microscope, and when he saw her standing there, the look he gave her was not very pleasant. "What are you doing here?" he growled under his breath. "Do you want to get me fired?"

"Oh keep your panties on." She quipped, then "We need to talk, can you take a break?"

He looked around and saw that he was being watched by a couple of co-workers. "C'mon" he said and took her by the arm heading toward the door. As he walked he told another worker "Mark, I'll be back in fifteen minutes, I'm taking my break."

Apparently Mark wasn't too happy with that because he quickly pointed out that it wasn't time to take a break.

Arnold looked angrily at Mark and snapped back "I don't take smoking breaks like half the other people in here so I guess it won't hurt if I take one fifteen minute break."

Kayla could tell that Mark was not used to being talked to like that and she was impressed with Arnold. She didn't think he had it in him. She smiled slyly as he led her out of the lab and down the hall. Soon, they were out in the parking lot and he led her to his car, a compact foreign car. He unlocked the doors with a push of a button, put her in the passenger's seat, and hurried around to the driver's seat.

From Kayla's car, Tom sat wondering what was going on.

Once he was in the car with the door closed, Arnold turned toward Kayla and said "Okay Kayla, what are you doing here?"

"I need some information from you." She answered.

"Oh you do huh?" she could tell he was angry "Why the hell should I give you anything? We had a deal, and you still owe me. I should have known that you wouldn't pay up." He looked almost ready to cry.

"Oh please, I thought you were the smart one here. I haven't taken care of my side of the agreement YET because I had to make absolutely sure that what you gave me was the right stuff. For all I knew, you could have given me a spray bottle of water. It took me a few weeks to find the perfect test subject and then I needed a couple more weeks to see if it actually worked." The expression on his face had completely changed from anger and hurt to hope.

"So did it work?" He asked.

"Like a charm. It works even better than I could have imagined." This was the hard part for her, but it was necessary. "Take out your cock Arnold."

Arnold's eyes got wide. "What…you want to do it here…now?"

"No time like the present. It's time I showed you that I'm a woman of my word." she reached across and slid her hand between his legs.

He looked around the parking lot, obviously very nervous. "Jesus Kayla what if someone walks by?"

"Are you going to take your cock out of your pants or what Arnold? I think he wants to come out." she was rubbing the rapidly swelling lump.

For a few uncertain moments, Arnold struggled with his worries, so Kayla gave him something else to think about, "Don't forget, you only have about ten more minutes." That got him moving. He lifted his ass up while unbuttoning his fly and awkwardly slid his pants down.

Kayla smiled at his nervousness and said, "You don't want me to suck you through you underwear now do you?"

Arnold looked at her with wide eyes, seemingly ready to pop out of his head, and then carefully slid down his underwear. He was shy and seemed embarrassed when his semi-hard penis flopped onto his thigh.

Kayla grinned widely and decided to give him a little encouragement. "Why Arnold, I do believe you've been holding out on me." She took his rapidly rising member into her hand and found that it was sweaty, or maybe it was her own palm that was sweaty, but either way, she was not looking forward to this. She steeled herself, then, licking her lips in an exaggerated sexy way, she leaned down real close and licked the very tip of his penis with the very tip of her tongue. It tasted salty and her nose was filled with his musky smell, but she pushed herself to continue.

Arnold's dick surged up with blood and was almost instantly fully erect. Standing up at about seven inches with a mushroom shaped head. She blew some cool air on it and giggled when it twitched. Then she sat back up.

Arnold looked almost ready to pass out and nearly yelled "Is that it? You call that a blow job?" he was shaking like a leaf and she hadn't done anything yet.

"Of course not Arnold. I just need one piece of information first. Tell me who manufactured my special scent and I'll suck you dry."

"AHH shit… it was uhh… it was Laura…Laura Stanwick, yeah that's right she had the fourth batch, the fourth group I mean, and she made yours."

Kayla hadn't even considered that it might be a woman and she was taken aback for a moment, but then she cleared her head and smiled. "Thank you, Arnold. Hope you like this." she leaned down again and took the head of his cock deep into her mouth, his taste nearly overpowering. She wanted to finish him off as quickly as possible, so she lifted up and dropped a big dollop of saliva on his shaft and stroked the lubed up base with her right hand while sucking gently and tickling just below his cock head with her tongue.

Kayla heard Arnold exhale loudly and felt him tense up almost immediately. He gripped the steering wheel with both hands and groaned. "Oh, shit oh fuck oh good god I'm cumming" and Kayla felt the first squirt fire into the back of her throat. She quickly pulled her head up and aimed his penis away from her face, inadvertently swallowing the sticky mess in the back of her throat. She hated the taste of semen and was not happy that he didn't warn her that he was going to shoot. He also came quicker than any guy she had ever sucked off before, under one minute.

She watched his face as he powered through his orgasm, his cum spraying all over the front of his shirt and some splashing his pants. His eyes were shut tightly, and his mouth was open in a big O shape. She had always thought that guys in the throes of orgasm made the funniest faces and this was proof. Before he was fully recovered, she slid back into her seat and checked her face in the mirror. Satisfied that she was clean, she opened the passenger door and climbed out, leaving Arnold gasping behind her. She hurried across the parking lot to her car and climbed in the driver's seat.

Chapter 6

"Damn it" she snapped "It's a fucking woman. Now what the hell am I going to do?"

Tom, who had been waiting in the passenger's seat was confused. "What are you talking about?"

Kayla sat silently for a thirty count, just thinking and finally sighed and said, "The person who made my batch of the designer scent is a woman."

"So, what does that have to do with anything?"

"Well, I was hoping it would be a man because men are so easy for a woman to manipulate. All we have to do is smile and flirt with them and they melt like butter."

Tom was about to object but thought better of it, instead he remained quiet.

"It's much more difficult for a woman like me to get another woman to do something. Unless she's a lesbian and she's single. I'm going to need your help, Tom. After we go see Dr. Hewes this afternoon, we need to get our hands on Laura Stanwick. She's the only one who can help you, Tom."

"What do you mean by 'help me'?" Tom inquired.

"We need someone to make more spray now don't we."

The rest of the day was spent making plans, both for when they went to see Dr. Hewes to how they would convince Laura Stanwick to make more stuff. They stopped at an Internet cafe and did some research on Laura. It wasn't too difficult to find a picture of her and even her address. With a plan in place, they headed back to Kayla's place.

By three o'clock, Tom was needing another fix. The time between fixes was getting shorter. With one hour left before the appointment, Kayla sprayed her pussy once more and felt the tingling. She was starting to enjoy how the spray made her feel more and more all the time and couldn't wait to get Tom's face down there. She laid on the bed with her knees hanging over the side and watched as he kneeled on the floor and dove in.

This time when he got down there, his eyes were once more drawn to her clit. He was sure that it was even bigger than this morning when he licked her under the table. He wasn't great with measurements, but he was sure that it was sticking out at least an inch and its thickness was close to a quarter. It was still partially concealed under her labia, but it was resembling a small penis more than ever. He also thought that her lips were thicker. He wanted to question her about it, but he smelled her scent, and he forgot. The only thing that he cared about was getting his fix.

He leaned in and pushed his mouth between her labia and breathed in her succulent aroma. His penis surged forward, filling with blood to an almost painful point. He slid his arms under her thighs and settled in when he felt her hands grab the back of his head and pull him tightly against her. Her super plump lips seemingly swallowing his face. His still sore nose was wedged up against her clitoris, which had elongated even more since he had started eating her. The pain in his nose was throbbing or maybe it was her giant clit that was throbbing, he couldn't be sure, but he was sure that he was going to ask her about it after he was done.

For Kayla, she realized at this point that she wanted pressure against her cunt and pulling his face into her was good, but she really wanted more. She wished that she could sit on his face again, but she was aware that his nose was broken, and she had promised him that if he helped her, she would make it easier on him. Holding his face tightly against her pussy would have to suffice for now. She was really enjoying the extra sensation that the spray seemed to be giving her. It was an unexpected plus. Not only did it seem to bring her to orgasm faster, but her orgasms seemed to be getting more powerful. She could feel every lick from Tom's tongue, and she just wanted to pull his whole head inside her.

Breathing had become a chore for Tom as his bruised nose was being blocked by Kayla's enormous clitoris. He was sticking his tongue as deep as he could inside her hole and licking all around it. If she hadn't been holding his head so tightly, he would have already moved to her clit, but she was waiting for the right moment to shift his mouth and that moment came just as he was completely out of air. As she pulled him up, he inhaled a deep breath through his nose and found his mouth stuffed full of her mini penis.

Her orgasm starting, Kayla wanted her clit sucked and moved his head to that spot. Feeling his mouth wrap around her clit, she thrust her pelvis forward and exploded. "AAAAAAAAAAAAAAAAAAAAAAAAAAHHHHHHHHHHHHHHHHHHHHHHH" her whole body went rigid as all her muscles locked. She involuntarily sat up and her heels dug into Tom's back. Meanwhile, her hands gripped the sides of his head so tightly, that his ears were completely plugged, and quite sore later. Her pussy started spraying his chin, she didn't even try to hold it back this time. Every part of her body was gripped in the throes of the most incredible orgasm she had ever felt. It was even better than the last one. Her cunt would spasm and stay contracted for up to fifteen seconds at a time before the contraction would release for about five seconds, and then spasm again. She didn't squirt the whole time though; she would have dehydrated if she had. Each time her pussy would start another spasm, more fluid would squirt for a second or two and she would scream in ecstasy. About forty-five seconds into her orgasm, she wondered if it would ever stop, if she would ever stop cumming. She would go mad with pleasure and eventually her heart would give out and she would die screaming and squirting and laughing hysterically. All in all, her entire orgasm lasted a full minute and twenty seconds before it finally stopped, and she fell back on the bed panting and sweating.

When Tom was released, he had one thought on his mind. His penis was ready to pop off. He was so horny, and he didn't wait for permission. He stood up and pushed himself deep into her puffed out pussy. It was like sliding into a soft blast furnace it was so hot, but it felt incredible, and he started pumping away like a man possessed. It only took him about forty-five seconds before he reached his apex and deposited his seed with a loud groan deep inside her sucking twat. Having exhausted himself, he dropped on top of her to catch his breath.

They laid together for five minutes catching their breath before Kayla looked at the clock and said "Shit, we need to get moving." it was twenty past three and they had to be at Dr. Hewes by four. They jumped up and rushed around taking a quick five-minute shower and getting dressed. Then they headed for her car.

Chapter 7

They arrived at Dr. Hewes office at 3:50. The receptionist, a young girl named Miranda that Tom guessed was about nineteen years old, smiled as they walked in and said "Good afternoon Mr. Jensen. I forgot that you were coming in this afternoon."

Tom smiled back at the pretty girl "Hi Miranda. I'd like you to meet my friend Kayla. She'll be sitting in my session with Dr. Hewes today."

Miranda glanced at Kayla, smiled and said a quick "Hi", then looked back at Tom. "You can have a seat and Marvin will be with you in a few minutes."

"Thanks" Tom said and went to the other end of the room to sit. Kayla sat next to him and quickly leaned in to whisper in his ear "Holy shit is she horny for you."

"What! She's just a kid, don't say that." Tom argued.

"Oh come on, she's not that young. I'll bet she's twenty years old, and I saw the way she looked at you. She thinks you're all that. Why don't you go talk to her, she's kinda cute."

Tom did agree that she was cute, he thought that from the first time he met her. She wasn't a typical beauty either and that somehow added to her attractiveness. She was short, about five foot three and she had short black hair in a boyish cut. Not typically what attracted Tom, but it worked with her cherub face. She kind of resembled a pin-up girl from the forties. She also had a nicely proportioned figure, not fat, but not a paper-thin waif either. Her lips and cheeks were plump and her perfectly straight teeth shined when she smiled, which was often. She also wore a tiny diamond on the side of her nose.

"Kayla, she's cute but she's too young for me. I'm nearly old enough to be her father." Tom said rather unconvincingly. He had slept with young ladies before, none under eighteen of course, but he didn't like to advertise it. It always made him feel sort of guilty. He was thirty-four years old after all. Maybe not ready to get married, but ready to start acting more his age.

"I'll handle this" Kayla stood up and walked up to the desk, leaving Tom wide eyed and wondering.

Miranda looked up at Kayla and smiled "Can I help you with something?" she asked.

Kayla used her most disarming smile and said "Well actually, I wanted to ask if I could get your opinion on something, you know, I need a ladies perspective."

"Oh sure" Miranda was only too happy to help.

"I just bought this new perfume" Kayla started, pulling the bottle out of her purse "and I want you to tell me what you think."

Tom saw the bottle come out and quickly stood up. He started to rush toward them intending to stop her, but he was too late as he saw Kayla quickly spray her wrist and hold it under Miranda's nose. "NO" he said quietly but forcefully.

Miranda, not focused on Tom, leaned in for a quick whiff and her expression changed instantly. Tom saw her eyes sort of gloss over and she immediately grasped Kayla's arm with both her hands, one on her wrist and one on her palm. She held the arm gently but firmly as she kept inhaling the scent over and over making mewling sounds. Her eyes seemed to get heavy and as Tom reached the desk he watched in dismay as Miranda actually licked the wrist. He pulled Kayla away and admonished her under his breath.

"What the hell do you think you're doing?" He whispered sharply. "Why would you do that?"

Kayla pushed him gently away replied "I know you want to fuck her, now you'll get your chance. If I decide to let you that is."

"Damn its Kayla, you can't do that."

"She'll do anything now to get her fix, just like you. Whatever I tell her to do."

Tom wanted to continue, but just then Dr. Hewes came out "Mr. Jensen, come on in.".

Looking back to the receptionist who was sitting with a peaceful look on her face, Tom turned toward the doctor and sighed deeply. He felt good right now because he had gotten his fix just an hour ago, so he wanted to drag Kayla out of there and berate her. However, he was worried about how he would feel later when the cravings started. The last thing he wanted right now was to piss her off. He stepped forward and said "Dr. Hewes, I'd like you to meet my friend Kayla."

Kayla stepped forward and offered her hand to shake. Shaking her hand Dr. Hewes said "So, are you the one who Tom is addicted to?"

Smiling sheepishly, Kayla shrugged, raised her eyebrows and said "Can you blame him doc?".

The good doctor laughed "Well come in and let's talk about it."

Chapter 8

As she walked into the room in front of Tom, Kayla pulled her V-neck shirt away from her chest and sprayed one squirt of the scent between her breast. No one else noticed because her back was to them.

Once in the room with the door shut, Kayla and Tom sat on the couch and Dr. Hewes sat in his leather chair. "So, Tom, tell me why you felt the need for another appointment so soon after our last one."

Tom looked at Kayla who nodded and then back to the doctor. "Well, I told you that I thought I was addicted to her," he motioned to Kayla "and I was right. She told me why I am addicted to her, and it's not at all what you thought."

The doctor nodded as if he completely understood and then asked "So Kayla, why don't you tell me what you told Tom."

Kayla stood up and said "Well, maybe it would be easier if I just showed you." she confidently strolled around to where Dr. Hewes was sitting and held her hand in front of him. "Would you stand up please."

For a moment, he looked at her with a quizzical expression, then she said, "Trust me, I won't bite." and he nodded and did as she asked.

Once he was standing face to face with Kayla he said "Okay, now what?". he glanced over her shoulder to look at Tom still on the couch and suddenly his vision was blocked as Kayla pulled her top off over her head. His shock was evident by the look on his face "What are you doing? Put your top back on miss." he was flustered but tried to remain professional.

Kayla just stood there in her bra smiling "Do you like what you see doc?" she asked. Then she reached up and unclipped the front latch and freed her rather ample breasts. "Sometimes it's nice to get that thing off, it can be rather restricting you know." she added.

The good doctor had seen enough "What is the meaning of this? Mr. Jensen will you please tell your lady friend to put her clothes back on and leave my office immediately." He had no idea what kind of stunt this was, but he was not amused. He started to turn away from her when she jumped into his arms, wrapping her legs around his waist and her arms around his head. He was so surprised that he fell backward, right into his leather chair. Kayla used this to her advantage and quickly slid up, so his face was right between her breasts. From there, she clamped her arms together on either side to trap his face.

As Dr. Hewes struggled to free himself from the assault, he became aware of a wonderful smell and even though he was frightened by this crazy woman, he soon calmed down and only wanted to breathe in her scent. It was heavenly and he wrapped his arms around her back and closed his eyes and kept breathing in her essence. He felt his cock getting hard in his pants and all thoughts of professionalism had left his head.

Kayla also felt his manhood growing under her ass. It felt too good to waste, so she started wiggling her hips back and forth. It took only a few minutes of her sliding her ass back and forth before the good doctor fired his load into his boxers.

After several minutes of Dr. Hewes breathing in the designer scent from between Kayla's tits, she finally disentangled herself from him and stood up. "Now you understand what Tom means. He wasn't lying to you doc. He really is addicted to me. You'll find out."

Still sitting in his chair, looking rather dishevelled now, Dr. Hewes looked back at Tom "What has she done to me?" he asked slightly out of breath.

Tom shrugged and said "The same thing she did to me doc."

Kayla walked over to Dr. Hewes desk and took a piece of paper and a pen and wrote down her address, and her cell phone number. Then she walked back to the doctor who seemed almost frightened of her. "You're going to need me in a few days. If I, were you, I'd come visit as soon as you start feeling the craving? You can try to resist, but you won't be able to." While she talked, she was putting her bra and shirt back on, then she turned to Tom and said, "Let's go, we have a woman to find." She headed toward the door but before she went out, she turned back to Dr. Hewes and said, "Oh and by the way doc, if you tell anyone about this, you won't get any more of what you're going to need."

As they walked back out into the waiting room, the pretty receptionist was still seated behind her desk looking a bit stoned. Kayla wrote down her number again and tucked it into Miranda's hand. Then she held her wrist in front of her again and let the girl breathe in her scent once more. As if in a drug induced high, the cute receptionist mewled sexily and started smelling and licking the wrist. Tom was fascinated and a little turned on by what he was watching. After a few minutes, Kayla pulled her hand away and grabbing Tom by the arm, marched toward the exit as if she were a mother leading a child.

Chapter 9

Later that evening they were parked in front of Laura Stanwick's house, and watched as she returned home from work. Laura was a tall athletic woman with long straight blonde hair and glasses. She was a forty-year-old divorced woman with a twenty-year-old daughter in college. Her friends would say she was married to her job, and after her first marriage ended badly, (she walked in on him having sex with two men) she had no desire to get married again.

Once inside the house, she turned on her stereo and slipped off her shoes. Walking barefoot into her bedroom, she took off her button up shirt and bra, then slipped a cut off tank top on. She then sat on the edge of the bed and pulled off her dress pants and panties and put on a pair of workout shorts. She then headed into the kitchen to get some bottled water, but was side-tracked by a knock at the front door.

Figuring that it was a friend of hers that sometimes went to the gym with her after work, she opened the door without first checking who was there. It wasn't her friend; it was a pretty red head. "Can I help you?" she asked, wondering what this woman was selling.

Kayla smiled sweetly "Hi, I'm so sorry to bother you but I was wondering if I could use your phone really quick, my car just quit running and I left my cell phone on the counter when I left earlier. If I could just call my brother, he's a mechanic and he live locally."

Laura, who stood eight inches taller and outweighed Kayla by sixty pounds, figured that she had nothing to worry about and stepped aside, welcoming her in. "I've been in the same predicament before, so I know how you feel. Come on in, the phone is over there on the wall."

"Thank you so much, I'll make it quick." Kayla replied as she made her way past the tall blonde. As Laura turned to follow, she saw movement out of the corner of her eye and turned back to the door to see a man coming in. The distraction was just enough for Kayla to turn back and place the Taser against the side of Laura's waist and shock her with enough voltage to drop her like a stone. She had never used her Taser before, so she wasn't sure what to expect. She liked what she saw.

To Laura, the shock from the Taser was like getting jabbed with needles over every inch of her body all at once. The pain was intense, as every muscle seized up, and she watched the floor rise up and slam her. She was still awake but disoriented and her body wouldn't work anymore. Even though the shock had passed, she couldn't control her extremities to get up let alone fight back.

Tom shut the door behind him and locked it. Then he tied Laura's arms together at the wrists while Kayla tied her legs. Then, he pulled her chin down and slid a ball gag into her mouth and strapped it behind her head. By the time she was regaining her faculties, she was securely restrained.

Kayla stood up over her and started to undress as she explained what was happening. "I'm really sorry that I shocked you like that, but I had no other choice. See we need you to do something for us and you probably won't want to." she dropped her shirt on the floor and unsnapped her bra.

Laura was freaking out thinking that she was going to be raped by a woman and a man and probably killed.

Unbuttoning her jean shorts Kayla continued "It's very important that you help us and the only way to make sure that you are going to help us is if you are in the same predicament that Tom over there is in. So…" she was naked now and she took the tiny spray bottle from Tom and held it up so Laura could see it. "I need you to make some more of this for me."

Laura knew exactly what was in the little bottle and her eyes grew wide with fear. She had been told that all samples had been destroyed. "MMMMMMMM" she tried to protest, shaking her head and trying to rise. This was not good, and it was obvious that these two didn't know what they were messing with.

Kayla raised her foot and placed it on Laura's chest, pushing her back down and holding her there.

Knowing that she had to tell them of the dangers, she tried to pull out the ball gag with her bound hands. She almost had it moved enough so she could talk around it too, but Tom grabbed her hands and pulled them over her head.

With Kayla standing the way she was, one foot on the floor and one on Laura's chest, her pussy was openly visible. Laura wasn't at all interested in looking at another woman's vagina, but when she did glance up, she couldn't miss the huge clitoris ballooning out. 'Oh my God' she thought 'she's been using it too much.'

For some reason this whole scene was exciting Kayla immensely. Standing naked over the bound woman, holding her down with one foot, she turned the bottle toward her spread vagina and pushed the plunger, once, twice, three times, then scooted her ass sideways and sprayed her ass two more times.

"What the hell, why did you use so much?" Tom questioned. He knew that the bottle would be running out soon and didn't know how long it would take to get more or if they would actually get more.

Kayla scowled at him as if she was angry that he would ask such a thing. "Don't worry about it, it's mine and I can use as much or as little as I want. Besides," she paused as tingling took over, she breathed in deeply and closed her eyes "OHHHH it feels so fucking good."

Tom looked at her crotch and saw how much larger her clit had grown. It was even longer and thicker than the last time. "Kayla, have you looked at yourself lately? Your clit is huge. What the hell is happening to you?"

Kayla smiled as she lowered herself down "I kinda like it. It's sooo sensitive. I can almost cum just from walking. The friction is marvellous". She dropped down to her knees with her moist vagina about an inch over Laura's face. Looking down into the eyes of the terrified woman under her made her even more horny. She could see that her captive was holding her breath and that made her laugh. "You might as well breathe because I can stay here all night."

Laura held her breath as long as she possibly could and when she couldn't last any longer, she tried twisting and pulling her arms away from Tom. It didn't work. With her head and chest pounding and her face turning purple, she finally let her breath go and inhaled the scent that she so desperately was trying to avoid. Defeated, she took several breaths. For several moments, while her adrenaline was still pumping, she was squirming and fighting. Soon however she realized just how wonderful the smell was and after a few minutes she wondered why she was so worried about it in the first place. The fact that she was not a lesbian and had never smelled another woman's pussy didn't matter to her anymore. She was in love with this woman's pussy and now she wanted to lick and suck it.

The whole scene was fascinating to Tom. He watched the terrified woman struggle and hold her breath until she was purple. It was almost as if she thought it was toxic. When she finally did succumb and start breathing through her nose, he saw her expression change from fear to calm. It took longer than the young receptionist in the doctor's office, but he figured that it was because the receptionist was already calm where Laura was struggling and fighting. Now though she looked serene, and he watched as she lifted her head off the floor to place her nose into the folds of Kayla's cunt and deeply inhale her aroma.

Kayla noticed the change too and when she felt the woman's nose sliding around her wet pussy, she slid back and looked her in the eyes. "I'm going to take off the ball gag but if you scream it will go back on. Understand?"

Laura nodded and lifted her head so to give easier access to the strap out back. When the latch on the gag was released and the ball was removed from her mouth, she said, "Thank you" and laid her head back on the carpet. Then, she looked back at Kayla and asked "Can I taste you? You smell so delicious, I want to lick you."

This was a first for Kayla. Never before had she done anything sexual with a woman. She had never wanted to do anything sexual with a woman because she was strictly heterosexual. However, she was so turned on at the moment that she didn't care who was between her legs, she was going to get off. She nodded and slid herself forward until her pumped up pussy was plastered on her face. She felt the softness of Laura's lips and tongue sliding around her labia and moaned deeply. It was so good, and her giant clit was up against her nose which added to the sensations.

Kayla was in her own little world of intense pleasure and she closed her eyes as she rocked her hips back and forth, riding Laura's face. Both women were moaning now, and Tom had slid his clothes off to join the fun. Walking around Kayla he moved to Laura's feet and untied her ankles and legs. Once she was untied, he moved up to her waist and started to pull her shorts down. At first, he wondered if she was going to struggle some more. He was not into rape, and even though he was very horny, if she protested, he would have stopped. He was somewhat surprised though when she lifted her butt off the floor to make it easier for him. As he started to pull them down, he also noticed just how wet she had become. The crotch of her shorts were soaked, almost as if she had urinated in them, but he could see that it wasn't urine at all. She was lubricating and had been before he had started to lower her shorts.

Once her shorts were down, she spread her legs wide and he watched in awe as she slid her still bound hands down and started to play with herself. Her pussy was beautiful, and he wanted taste it, so he got down on his hands and knees between her outstretched legs and lowered his face down. He could hear her fingers squelching in the soft, wet folds of her vagina. He inhaled her luscious sex smell and felt his penis twitch in excitement. He reached out and gently moved her hands up while leaning in and licking from her anus to her clit. He felt her tense up and shiver and then her fingers grasped his hair and pulled his face back into her moist folds.

Meanwhile, Kayla was nearing her orgasm and decided that she wanted her clit sucked. Tilting herself forward, she placed her enormous sex organ on Laura's soft lips and said "Open". Dutifully, the intoxicated woman opened wide and allowed the giant clit inside her sucking mouth.

"OOOOOOOHHHHHHHYYYEEEEEEESSSSS" Kayla cried as she felt as she felt smooth, velvety soft lips and tongue caress her swelling, sensitive nub.

To Laura, it was almost as if she was sucking on a small cock. In the deepest part of her mind, she knew what was happening was wrong. She knew that she was under the influence of the spray that was applied in excess just minutes earlier, and she also knew that the spray was changing the body of the woman who sat atop her. It was an unintended consequence of the liquid and no one really understood why it happened or just how far it would go. The other test subjects had been cut off cold turkey when it was discovered that there were changes starting on a genetic level. Once the spray had been stopped, their bodies reverted back to normal, but it was speculated that continued use could cause permanent changes. She was also aware that her exposure meant that she was very likely addicted and would have to go through a detox program to clean her system out. All of this and more was in the back of her mind somewhere but at the moment she didn't care. At the moment she only felt bliss. At the moment she only felt love for the two strangers who had tricked her, shocked her, tied her up and gagged her.

Her pleasure was rising higher than ever before. The tongue tickling her pussy was ravishing her, sending her closer to nirvana. The spongy mass of nerve endings that she was currently bathing in her saliva and being played with by her tongue, was throbbing hotly between her lips. She could hear slurping and moaning and grunting, all sounds that were heightening the experience. She was looking up the slightly flabby belly to the undersides of hanging breasts. At some time, she didn't know when, her hands had been untied and she was now caressing the ample ass that was over her head. The smell of sex in the air was overwhelming. All five senses were combining to send her over the top.

Kayla was the first one to reach her peak and cum. Her orgasm started at her clitoris and spread through her belly and thighs and all through her body. Lately her orgasms were not only much more intense, but they were also lasting much longer than ever before. The muscles in her vagina would clench as her pleasure became overwhelming and the clenching would go on and on. The feelings radiated outward to every inch of her body and all her muscles would tighten. Her toes splayed wide, her hands became claws and then fists, her face had a look of almost pain, but it wasn't pain at all that she was feeling, it was incredible pleasure. This orgasm lasted for a full minute while she moaned and humped, clenched and sweated and finally shook like she was shivering.

Sometime during the intensity of Kayla's wild orgasm, Laura started her own orgasm. She spit out the massive clit in her mouth and wailed through her own pounding cascade of joy, bouncing her bottom up and down off the floor while Tom tried to stay with her. It was a magnificent orgasm that lasted twenty seconds, but paled in comparison to Kayla's. As she came down from her orgasmic high, she realized that the pussy over her face was still contracting and throbbing. She also noticed that a white thick mucus like substance was dripping out of the vaginal cavity and her chin and neck were slimy from it. Her clouded mind didn't care, in fact, it heightened the whole experience for her.

As Kayla's orgasm started to subside, she realized that she hadn't had a cock in her for quite a while, so she turned herself around, so she was still kneeling over Laura's face but now facing her feet, and said "Tom, I need your cock inside me. Come fuck me."

Tom didn't need to be told again. His penis was swollen so much it was almost painful to touch. He quickly hurried around behind Kayla and kneeled between her spread legs. His knees were right up against Laura's head and he looked down into her lusty eyes as he lined up his erection with Kayla's pussy. As he slid into her cavern, he was struck by the heat. For some reason, her pussy felt much hotter than any other pussy he had ever fucked. The feeling was incredible, and he grabbed her thighs and started pumping his seven-inch penis in and out. The sound that she made when he started fucking her was almost inhuman. He couldn't believe how wet her cunt was and the sounds that his manhood made sliding in and out of her were almost funny. Squelching and sucking sounds, like pulling your boot out of thick mud. She was so wet that she was dripping creamy liquid on Laura's forehead.

Laura, while still recovering from her wonderful orgasm, was watching intently the action going on right in front of her eyes. It was an amazing sight from this close. The thick smell of pussy juice was so strong that she could taste it. Her own hands were between her legs lazily playing with herself. She wished there was another cock to stuff into her pussy.

The cock sliding in and out of Kayla's hot pussy was sending her into fits, but she wanted more. Something that she had never tried before was anal sex. She used to think it would be way too painful and therefore never tried it. Now however, it sounded like just what she needed to take her to the next level. She twisted her head to the side and said "I want it in my ass. Fuck my asshole, Tom." she then looked back down and saw Laura playing with herself and decided that she wanted a taste of that too. As she felt Tom slide his member out of her sucking cunt, she was pulling Laura's hands out of the way, and as she felt the swollen head of Tom's cock begin it's push against her anal sphincter, she lowered her face down into Laura's pulsing pussy and started to lick.

Anal sex was new to Tom too. He had never had the opportunity to try it with any of the women he had fucked. As he placed the head of his throbbing penis against her puckered hole, he thought to himself that there is no way it was going to fit. He had seen porn videos of girls getting their asses fucked and it always looked like you could drive a truck up their ass. This was way different. This asshole was very tight. He pushed slowly and felt the opening start to expand and suddenly the mushroom head popped inside. It was an amazing feeling, much different from fucking a pussy, and he only had the head in. He heard Kayla gasp and he paused, wondering if he had hurt her, but then she said, "YES FUCK ME." and he pushed forward, burying half of his seven inches in his first thrust.

"OOOOOOOHHHHHHHHHHHFFFFFUUUUCCCKKKKMMMMMEEEEEE" Kayla wailed in delight as she felt the fleshy shaft invade her most secret region. It felt wonderful and she wished that she had tried it sooner. She thought after the first thrust that he was all the way inside her, but when her pulled out and thrust in again, deeper this time, she wailed again. It was about this time when her legs and arms became weak. She lowered herself down until her sloppy pussy was resting on Laura's face and her own face was back in Laura's. Both women, in the throes of a blissful sexual high, started licking each other's pussies.

It took three strong thrusts from Tom to sink his raging hard on all the way into Kayla's bowels. Once his hips were planted up tight against her plump ass cheeks, he paused to relish the feeling. His pause wasn't long however because Kayla started rocking her ass back and forth and he took the hint. Soon he was thrusting as hard as he could, slamming her ass with each plunge forward and sending her body ahead several inches. He would pull his cock almost all the way out, until just the head was still inside, and then drive himself forward on his powerful legs, making a slapping sound. Each thrust caused both ladies to grunt like animals. After about thirty strokes, Tom was unable to hold back anymore, and he gripped her thighs tightly and yelled "AAAAARRRRRRRRGGGGGGGHHHHHHHH" as his semen burst forth from his throbbing member and sprayed deeply into her rectum.

Kayla was on the verge of another orgasm herself when she felt Tom's cock ram all the way in and stop. Then, with her clit being sucked by Laura, she heard his animalistic cry and felt his scalding hot cum blasting deep inside her gut. That was enough to set her off and she felt the familiar spasms starting as her own orgasm overtook her. It was another outrageously strong one and this time her pussy sprayed a jet of juices like she was urinating. She didn't try to hold it back, she couldn't if she wanted to, and it sprayed like a hose. This time she closed her eyes and rode through wave after wave after wave of spasms that went on and on. Twenty-three spasms altogether and by the end she was so spent she was nearly unconscious.

As for Laura, she had her own mini orgasm that was somewhat ruined by the sudden blast of spray from Kayla's pussy. She wasn't expecting to be pissed on and although it wasn't technically piss, it was like getting pissed on. She found herself nearly drowning as the spray blasted up her nose and down her throat. With all of Kayla's weight on top of her and Tom leaning over the top, she was unable to move and just had to endure it.

The experience for Tom was quite intense. Whole he was fucking Kayla's ass, her sphincter loosened up quite a bit, although it was still pretty tight. Then he started cumming and his cock swelled up even bigger as he started pumping his seed into her. Almost immediately after that, she started to cum also and that's when things got interesting for him. When Kayla reached her orgasm, her spasms caused her sphincter muscle to tighten up extremely tight. Because his cock was balls deep inside her at the time, it was as if someone had tightened a cock ring on him and his second blast of cum was held in. It wasn't painful exactly, but instead of him shooting his load and finishing his orgasm in about twenty seconds, her tight muscles caused his orgasm to be extended while the cum dribbled out slowly between her spasms.

By the time they all stopped cumming and grinding and moaning, all three were exhausted and Tom rolled off onto the floor to catch his breath. Kayla rolled to the other side and closed her eyes, and Laura lied where she was trying to clear her muddled head. Within minutes, all three were fast asleep.

Chapter 10

Thirty minutes passed with all three naked people lying together on the floor before Laura woke with a start and sat straight up. She looked at the two people sleeping on both side of her and had to stifle a cry of despair. The smell of sex was still hanging in the air and she was coated in dried cum and sweat. She remembered what had happened vividly and was angry and embarrassed with herself. Carefully and quietly as she could be, she extracted herself and tiptoed out of the room and into the bathroom where she looked the door. She sat on the toilet and pissed and then turned the shower on. Soon she was washing all the evidence of her earlier exploits off her body.

Tom woke next and sat up. It took him a moment to remember where he was and what had happened. He looked at Kayla still sleeping and realized that Laura was gone. That was when he heard the shower turn on in the bathroom and got up. He made his way to the bathroom door and walked in, closing the door behind him. He didn't bother waiting for an invitation, he just climbed in the shower behind her. She stiffened visibly when she saw him and moved her arms to cover her private areas.

"It's a little late for modesty don't you think." Tom said with a slight smirk. He reached around her for the bottle of body wash, not caring that it was lavender and obviously for women.

"You people have no idea what you've done." she said shivering, her brow furrowing with a look of dismay.

"Hey, you're the one who made the shit in the first place. Besides, I was a victim before you. I've been addicted to that shit now for weeks."

Laura looked away in shame or disgust, he wasn't sure which. Then said "Look, the formula wasn't mine in the first place. I was just a lab worker doing my job. It was an experimental formula, and when they found out just what the shit does, they ordered it all destroyed. How the hell did she get it in the first place?"

"I guess she promised some nerd a blowjob if he smuggled out her sample. Apparently, it was the dude who was supposed to destroy it."

"Peters, Arnold fucking Peters. That little shithead is a fucking male chauvinist pig. He hits on anyone with a pulse."

"Don't hold back now, tell me what you really think of him." Tom joked.

She actually smiled. It was a quick split-second smile, but it was a smile. "Listen, the shit that she has is bad shit. You've seen the changes in her body, I heard you comment about her clit, how big it is. It's hideous. The women in the first study group were only using the spray for two weeks. They were using the spray on their chest and each one saw growth of their nipples. At first it was thought that only the people who smelled them became addicted, but after the tests were halted, all of the women came back within two days complaining that they were fidgeting, agitated, tense, irritable, stressed out. They were experiencing withdrawal symptoms just like the others. These women were spraying it on their chests, and they were addicted to the feelings it gave them in their chests. She was spraying her vagina. That's mucous membrane which will affect her much stronger. There's no telling what will happen to her, let alone you for staying with her for so long."

"Look, when I started to realize that something wasn't right, I told my psychologist about her and he told me to breathe through the cravings. He thought it was in my head and I would get over it. I couldn't even make it through the night before I had to see her again."

"We need to get help, for her and us. We can't let her make us breathe anymore of that stuff. It needs to be destroyed. The sooner the better. When we get out of here, we need to get that bottle and get her to the lab. We all need to be in detox."

Tom knew she was right, and he agreed with her. He knew that he couldn't continue to live like he was, and he was aware that he had been getting worse. A week ago, he never would have agreed to do what he had done tonight.

What neither one of them knew was that Kayla was standing outside the shower listening to everything. When she heard the water turn off, she stepped back out to the other room to wait for them.

Chapter 11

Tom exited the bathroom first and never saw Kayla who was up against the wall by the door. She waited for Tom to pass and when Laura walked out, she shocked her from behind with the Taser. Tom heard the crackling zap and Laura's cry and spun around as she fell to the floor. "Tie her up Tom." she ordered. "Make sure her hands are behind her back. Tie her legs at the ankles, run the rope up through her wrists and pull it tight to make sure she can't run."

Tom was incredulous. "Kayla, what the hell are you doing?"

"I heard you two talking in there. She wants to take us back to the lab so they can help us. Tom, if they get their hands on us it will be the last time, you'll see me. They will keep us separated." She grabbed his arm to make him look her in the eyes. "You'll never get to fuck me again, or eat me, or smell me. Do you want that?"

He knew what had to be done. He was aware that he was hopelessly addicted and there was no telling how far it would go. He knew that he needed help and Laura could get him that help, but as he looked into Kayla's eyes, he was struck by how beautiful she was. She was more than a woman, she was a freshly fucked goddess. She was an angel without wings. She was all he needed.

"Now, are you going to tie her down or what?" Kayla asked. She had seen the look on his face soften when he looked into her eyes and she knew that she had him again. It had been close and if she hadn't woken when she did, it would probably be all over, but he nodded and quickly got to work securing Laura.

He had her arms tied securely behind her back and was working on her legs when she started to come to. Even though she was aware what was happening she was still unable to do anything about it. She could talk, however. "Wha…what…nooo don't please…we need help. Stop it." He was now pulling her legs back and wrapping the rope between her hands. "This is wrong. We need to get to the lab right away. Please untie me."

From the bathroom he heard Kayla say, "Put the ball gag on her Tom." She was washing up and getting dressed.

Tom grabbed the ball gag while Laura whined "Please no, please you can't do this ahhhmm". With the ball gag in place, she was no longer able to protest. Tom looked into the bathroom and asked, "Now what do we do?"

"Well, now I'll have to work on getting her more compliant. If she doesn't agree to make what we need, maybe we'll have to bring in her daughter to give her some incentive."

Laura, upon hearing that they would bring her daughter into this, started freaking out "MMMMMMMMMMMMMMMMMMMM" she yelled through her gag twisting and squirming.

Kayla walked back into the room fully dressed and got on the floor next to Laura. "Now don't worry" she assured "I don't really want to bring your daughter here. All you need to do is help me to get more of this…" she held up the bottle again which was now about a third full "and all will be fine.' She stood up and turned back to Tom, "Let's get her in the car, we're going to take her to the lab."

"What good is that going to do? She's not going to do what you want."

"Let me worry about that, you just do what I tell you to do."

Chapter 12

It took a bit a wrangling and there was the worry of someone seeing what was happening, but luckily it was getting dark out and Kayla backed the car right up close to the door. Once Tom got Laura in the car (she was kneeling on the floor in the back seat facing Kayla) he got in the driver's seat and headed toward the lab.

Once they were on the road, Kayla took her spray bottle and held it up, looking at it "Let's see now, what body part should I make you smell this time hmm?" She looked at Laura who was shaking her head and obviously very uncomfortable. "You've already been between my legs. Maybe you'd like to be between my breasts hmm."

she pulled her shirt up to show her hanging breasts. Laura noticed her swollen nipples. They looked as if they had been pumped up and they appeared to be very sensitive. "Come to think of it, I've already had someone between my breasts today, and he really enjoyed my special smell too."

'My God' Laura thought 'she's done it to someone else'.

"Maybe you like feet huh. Are you one of those freaks that like to sniff people's smelly feet? I could spray my feet and you could smell them. Would you like that?" she caressed Laura's cheek thinking to herself how uncomfortable she must be hogtied like she was. "No wait, I know just the thing." she lifted her left arm over her head and sprayed once into her armpit as if it was a can of deodorant. Then, dropping the spray bottle onto the seat she grabbed Laura's head and maneuvered herself until she had her face in her pit. It was a struggle but not a big one.

It was another degradation for Laura, the thought of smelling her armpit kind of turned her stomach but she had no leverage to struggle, and she could only hold her breath for about twenty seconds before she once again succumbed and started to breath in the unpleasant odour of pit sweat. Kayla knew that her underarms smelled bad as she had intentionally not washed them earlier. It was all part of her plan.

For Laura the smell was really bad, but there was another smell also that she craved so much. Once she got a whiff of that underlying scent, she didn't care about the bad sweat smell anymore. Her tenseness melted away and she inhaled deeply, and, on her exhale, she moaned into the ball gag.

"Oh there there, that's it. You like my pit sweat don't you. You really are a kinky bitch. You can just stay right there and keep breathing it all in until we get where we are going."

It was degrading and humiliating on one level for Laura, but that didn't matter right now. What mattered was the feeling of euphoria her body felt that she did not want to ever stop.

"You like that don't you? Yeah, I can see by the look in your eyes that you just love it. Too bad that I'm going to run out soon and you'll never be able to feel this way again. Unless you can make some more. You made the first batch, so you can make more. You can make as much as you want, so you can feel this good whenever you want. Do you want to feel this good again?"

Laura's mouth and nose were buried in odiferous arm pit but her eyes were staring into Kayla's almost lovingly and when she was asked if she wanted to feel like this again, she nodded and her eyes seemed to smile.

"So you are going to be able to make more right?"

Once more she nodded.

"Good, I just knew that you were going to be able to help." Then Kayla came up with another idea. "If you agree to be my personal slave, I'll let you feel this way all the time. You'd like that wouldn't you?" More nodding "Good girl. We are almost there so I'm going to untie you now."

In the next five minutes, Laura was untied, and Tom was pulling into the parking garage by the lab. He used Laura's pass card to open the gate then followed the signs to the third level where the lab was located and parked. The lot was nearly deserted because of the hour.

They gained entrance to the building with Laura's pass card and into the lab with the seven-digit pass code. A few years ago, they would have had to deal with security guards, but when the economy tanked the company laid them off and now relied solely on the security system. Only some of the workers had access to the building after hours and occasionally lab workers would stay late to finish an important project. This night there was no one else there and Laura got to work.

Kayla stayed close to Laura and when her attitude seemed like it was changing, she would spray some more of the scent on her body and let her smell it to keep her in line. It was a very efficient system and approximately three hours later, the new batch of designer scent was ready. This time it was a large bottle. It was just in time too because the small bottle was nearly empty.

Kayla took the large bottle and sprayed her chest once then called over Tom to make sure that it would work. She felt the warm tingling before he even got to her and when he leaned in to breathe her scent, she saw his face change and she knew that it was the right stuff. She was feeling horny again and really wanted to play, but she knew that they had already taken enough chances and they needed to leave. They spent the next twenty minutes cleaning up and putting everything back in order and finally Kayla felt confident that everything was back to normal. She knew that if anyone at work noticed anything out of the ordinary, management would check the video cameras and they would be in serious trouble. As long as nothing was noticed, in one week the video would be recorded over, and they would get away with it. Kayla also figured that by the time the big bottle was running out, Laura would be so highly addicted that she would find a way to make more at work and not get caught.

Back in the car, Kayla and Laura sat in the back seat again while Tom drove home. Kayla striped her pants off and sprayed her pussy with the new bottle, then grabbed Laura by the hair and pulled her roughly down. "Lick my pussy, make me cum." The tingling sensation started up and her clitoris filled with blood, now nearly as long as her thumb.

She pulled her clit up and guided Laura's mouth below that, moaning lustily as she felt the soft tongue licking up her wet pussy. Wrapping two fingers and a thumb lightly around her elongated clit, she started stroking it up and down just like a man would stroke his penis. She quickly brought herself to the brink of orgasm and then let out a scream as she was pushed over the edge and her pussy burst. Once again, a jet of clear fluid squirted into Laura's mouth stinging the back of her throat and causing her to pull back and go into a fit of coughing.

While Laura coughed, Kayla was shaking and moaning and cumming. She looked down and saw that her clit was not only standing up straight, but it was also throbbing, bulging and looking more than ever like a cock. The more she rubbed it, the longer her orgasm lasted, until she had to let go because it was too sensitive. When she did let go, it twitched for another twenty seconds or so while she lost control of her muscles and went limp in the seat, gasping for breath, her heart racing as she rode the slowly fading wave to the very end.

As Laura got control of her coughing, she watched the last of Kayla's orgasm and was amazed and a little frightened. Meanwhile, in the front seat, Tom could barely keep his mind on the road as he drove the car back to Laura's house.

Chapter 13

When they arrived at the house, Kayla realized that Laura couldn't be trusted to be left alone all night. When her mind cleared up, she would likely call for help. At the moment though, Laura was still under the influence of the scent and would do whatever she was told. "Tom," she paused as she weighed her words a "we will be staying here for a few days with Laura to make sure that she doesn't try to get help. I want to tie her up so I can sleep without worrying that she is going to sneak away in the night. Let's tie her to that chair over there and put the ball gag in her mouth so she can't start screaming."

Tom went to work taking Laura by the hand and leading her to the wooden chair. As he was getting the rope ready though, Kayla stopped him. "Wait, I want you to take her clothes off first. Everything except her underwear."

Tom nodded and started helping her strip. She was not so much in a trance as she was just super compliant. He wondered what she would do if he told her to jump out the window or stab herself with a knife. It was kind of frightening to think about. Soon she was nearly naked and sitting in the cold wooden chair. It had to be uncomfortable, but she didn't seem to mind being tied tightly to it. He made sure that she wasn't going to get loose by using plenty of rope, but he also didn't tie it too tightly so her circulation would be cut off. He spread her legs to either side and tied her knees to each arm, along with her ankles to each leg. Her arms were tied around the wrists, elbows and upper arms. Then he went around her waist, belly and chest several times to make sure. Lastly, he slipped the ball gag in her mouth and strapped it around the back of her head.

As Tom finished up with Laura, he turned around to see Kayla topless and spraying her breasts with the new bottle. Just seeing the bottle now made him start to perspire and fidget. Kayla saw him staring at her and she motioned him to her. He didn't wait to be asked again and practically ran around the coffee table to get to her. He buried his face between her breasts thinking that he they seemed bigger than normal for some reason, and the wonderful aroma of her skin, sweat, and the spray that she had sprayed on that didn't actually smell like anything, assaulted his senses and he drifted into a drug induced stupor.

Kayla's breasts were super sensitive now and her erect nipples were as hard as pencil erasers and as big as thimbles. She held Tom's head gently between her breasts while he breathed deeply, inhaling all he could of her, and becoming more willing to please her with every breath. She waited a few minutes for him to get plenty of what he needed and then she decided to get what she wanted.

"Tom dear," she whispered, pulling his face up close to hers "I want you to do something for me. Will you do something for me Tom?" she was staring intently into his eyes, her eyes flicking back and forth from his left eye to his right.

"Will you lick my asshole again? I loved it so much the last time, and if you will do that for me, I'll let you fuck me in the ass. How's that sound huh? Does that sound like fun to you Tom? Would you like to fuck my tight little asshole, Tom? I've never had a cock in my asshole before. I want you to take my anal cherry Tom. Will you do that for me?" she leaned in and kissed him, opening her mouth, turning her head to the side and pushing her tongue deep into his mouth to lick his tongue. She was also rubbing her body up against his body and she could feel his hard cock straining to get out of his pants.

She kissed him for several minutes, getting them both heated even more if that was possible, and while she did, she was pulling his and her clothes off. Once they were both naked, she pulled him down onto the floor, so he was kneeling, then she laid in front of him on her back. Her long clitoris stood straight up in the air. She reached under her thighs and lifted her legs up, bending her knees and rolling up on her upper back, which lifted and rolled her ass up to give him easy access.

He crawled forward and looked down at her puckered pink orifice. Her ass was really beautiful, now that he was staring at it like this and when he lowered his face down close, he could smell just a hint of unpleasantness. She was obviously a very clean woman, and he wasted no more time, starting by licking all around on her soft pillowy cheeks. As he got closer to the skin around her opening, he heard her uneven breathing and knew that it was having an effect on her.

Kayla had basically folded herself in half with her legs spread wide and her elbows in the crease under her knees. This left her wide open and she could see exactly what was going on. She pulled her enormous clit down and realized that in this position, it almost reached her mouth. From her perspective, she could see the tip of Tom's nose hovering over her open pussy, but she couldn't see his mouth working on her asshole. She could definitely feel his tongue working all around her sensitive opening, making it even more sensitive and when she started putting pressure on her engorged clit/penis by gripping it between her thumb and forefinger, she was well on her way to an explosive orgasm. "Put your tongue in my asshole." she groaned, wishing he would just do it already. Then she squealed as she felt him pushing it in.

With his tongue driving into her anal opening, Tom was looking right into Kayla's pussy. Her impossibly long clit was throbbing between her fingers and pussy juice was bubbling up from her clenching cunt. The smells, sounds and sights of everything going on was incredibly erotic and he was unable to keep his hands off his own raging hard on.

Meanwhile, Laura was watching all of the blistering excitement from her perch on the chair and was unable to play with her needy pussy. She was horny and frustrated and on the verge of a breakdown. She wished they would untie her so she could join in, but little did she know, Kayla had plans for her.

Speaking of Kayla, her body was now quaking like leaf on a windy day, and she was awash in a sheen of sweat as she approached the pinnacle of pleasure. She yelled over and over "OHYEAHOHHHSHITOOOOFUCKMEEEEEEEE!!!!" and Tom, upon hearing that, wasted no time. He stood up and wedged his mushroom shaped penis head between her moist, plump ass cheeks, and with one huge lunge, he shoved his throbbing shaft balls deep into her rectum.

Kayla, who had been so into the pleasure that she hadn't even realized what she had said and really wasn't ready to be impaled in her ass, let out a yowl like a cat in heat "EEEEEEEEEAAAAAAAHAHHHHHHHHHHHH" and the shock and the savagery of the thrust sent her into spasms of orgasm like she had never experienced before. It felt like everything below her breasts and above her knees tightened up for several seconds before she let loose.

With his cock buried to the hilt, Tom felt her sphincter tighten up so much he couldn't pull himself back out. It was so tight that it was almost painful, and he was so alarmed that he pulled back and only succeeded in lifting her up three inches before he dropped back down. His orgasm started then, it was basically pulled out of him by her incredibly tight ass. However, for the first several seconds, the base of his penis was so tightly clenched that no semen was released. This caused him to swell even larger as just a small dribble of cum leaked out the tip. The pleasure mixed with the pain and added to the intensity. He opened his mouth and let out a yell of his own as his balls worked extra hard to expel the sperm. "SSSSHHHHHHIIIIIIIITTTTTT" he screamed thinking for a moment that he was going to lose his penis but still caught in the pleasure of his orgasm.

Finally, things loosened up as Kayla's whole body was wracked by her climax and her spasms started. Juices, thick and creamy bubbled and spurted up from her clenching pussy and ran down the crease between her thigh and her belly. Still holding on to her clit, she could feel it pumping like a piston with every spasm. For a moment, in her euphoria, she thought it was leaking juices too, but she really didn't believe that. There were juices spraying all over the place, so it was just an illusion. After all, it wasn't a penis, it was a clitoris.

It took nearly five minutes for the two of them to calm down and catch their breath and by that time they looked up at Laura, she was panting heavily and squirming her butt around, as if she was trying to get some kind of pressure, any pressure on her sexual organs.

Tom spoke first "So what are we going to do with her, leave her like that all night?"

Kayla could see that she was struggling "Not quite like that," she answered "I've got a few ideas to help her get through the night."

Fifteen minutes later she was still in the same position, but she was squirming, panting and sweating even more than before and Tom finally realized how sadistic Kayla really was.

She had obviously put a lot of thought into what she had done. First, she had picked up her discarded underwear and sniffed them, pulling them away from her face quickly and making a face of disgust as they apparently had a very strong odour. She then used them to mop up her sopping wet pussy and ass, making a sloppy, sticky mess on her panties. She then picked up her new bottle of designer scent and sprayed the underwear once.

"That should mix with my smell and work just as well as if I sprayed myself." she said to Tom. She then pulled the soiled panties over Laura's head, making sure the slimy, sticky mess was right over her nose. They both watched as she started breathing the smell in and she seemed to visibly clam down.

Tom assumed she was done but she wasn't. She next went to her purse and dug down to the bottom, pulling out a rabbit style vibrating dildo. Holding it up for Tom to see she said, "I just put in brand new batteries so it should last a long time." The dildo was an expensive one with beads and a clitoral stimulator. She reached down and pulled Laura's panties to the side then carefully slid the thick dildo all the way into her pussy until the clitoral stimulator was up against her clit. Satisfied with its placement, Kayla turned it on and pulled the crotch of her panties back over it so it wouldn't slide out. The buzzing could be heard throughout the room and Laura jumped and her eyes opened wide, visible through the leg openings of the panties.

"There" Kayla stepped back to admire her handiwork "that ought to keep her happy. At least for a while anyway." Then she turned back to Tom, "Let's go to bed, I'm exhausted." she turned and headed to the bathroom to wash up.

For a few moments, Tom stood looking at Laura, who was making mewling sounds through the ball gag and seemed visibly more uncomfortable than before, then he followed Kayla to the bathroom. In ten minutes, they were in Laura's bed with the lights out.

Chapter 14

The next morning, Tom woke early and after clearing his head and remembering where he was, he carefully slid out of bed and tiptoed out of the room. He was confident that Kayla was still sleeping. When he walked into the living room, he could still hear buzzing, although it was much quieter than it had been the night before, or at least he thought it was. He found Laura, still tied in the chair, but she looked much worse for the wear. As he quietly moved into the room, he thought she was sleeping because her head was tilted sideways, and her eyes looked like they were shut. However, when he stepped around in front of her, her eyes popped open wide, and she looked up to him.

That was when he saw the mess. Her chair and the floor around the chair was wet with piss and other juices. It was quite obvious that she had been drooling all over herself and she was covered in sweat. Her eyes were bloodshot, and she was trembling all over. She looked like she was a wild, rabid animal.

Tom felt bad for her and immediately moved to take off her ball gag. The smell near her was awful and he scrunched his face as he pulled the underwear off her head and unlatched the ball gag. Carefully he pulled it out of her mouth and heard her whisper "water". He quickly rushed to the kitchen, not trying to be quiet anymore and opened cupboards until he found a glass. He filled the glass in the sink and rushed it back in. As he brought it close to her, he noticed her squirming her bottom around as much as the bindings allowed and she was huffing and puffing like a pregnant woman. He was confused for a moment until he realized that she was suffering through an orgasm.

He set the glass down and hurriedly pulled her panties to the side so he could pull the vibrator out of her abused pussy. It was covered in slime and still buzzing away, and he tossed it onto the couch. Her poor pussy looked red and raw and was still pulsating. He grabbed the glass of water again and held it up to her dry lips so she could drink. She seemed to revive somewhat as she gulped the cool liquid down. He let her drink half the glass then pulled it away saying, "Slow down, you don't want to throw up."

She looked up into his eyes and seemed to smile a bit. "Thank you." she whispered. Then "Can you untie me please? I can't feel my legs."

Tom exhaled loudly then looked to the bedroom door. He half expected to see Kayla staring angrily at him, but the door was still shut. "Yeah, yes I uh…of course." He busied himself untying the knots that he had secured the night before and when he finished, he helped her over to the couch. He was feeling bad for his involvement and for the moment his mind was clear, so he sat next to her and quietly spoke to her. "Listen, we should get some help, this is all wrong. Kayla is too far gone. That stuff…it's changing her, just like you said. We need to get out of here and get help."

He really thought that after a long night tied to an uncomfortable chair with a vibrator buzzing away in her pussy, she would be more than ready to escape. "We need to get you cleaned up and get out of here." he continued. "If we go back to the lab, they should be able to get us the help we need. Let's go clean up." he took her by the arm and helped her get to her feet, then led her to the bathroom. Once in the bathroom with the door closed, he started the shower and after peeling her soaked panties off her, he helped her into the shower and climbed in with her.

There were deep marks around her arms and thighs where the ropes had bit in during the night and he gently washed her whole body from her head to her toes. He was trying to stay focused on the task at hand and had to clear his mind several times when he was washing her body. She was after all a very sexy woman and he was running his hands over every inch of her wet body. It took discipline, which at this point he knew was scarce in him, but he did manage to get her clean and only became semi hard during. Then he moved her away from the water so he could wash himself.

Once they were out and dried up, Tom helped Laura get her clothes on and got himself dressed. Then, he opened the bathroom door and looked at the bedroom door which was still closed. Thinking Kayla must still be asleep, he helped Laura over to the front door. Before he could open the door however, Laura stopped him. "Wait, we need the car keys."

Tom had been so intent on getting out of the house that he forgot all about car keys. "Shit" he exclaimed and headed for the bedroom. Before he could go in though, Laura stopped him again.

"I should get them." she started "The floor creaks in certain spots, really loud if you step in the wrong place. I can avoid it and be quieter."

It sounded reasonable to Tom and he nodded "Yeah, your probably right. Just be very quiet."

"Of course" she smiled and headed toward the closed door. Tom watched her as she quietly opened the door and was glad it didn't squeak. He didn't bother to go over next to the bedroom door, just waited by the entryway and contemplated their next move. He waited nearly five minutes thinking about what would happen to them all and then realized that it was taking her way too long. He quickly headed over toward the bedroom door but before he could get there Laura came back out holding the keys.

"Shit," he exclaimed in a whisper, "What took so long?"

She walked over to him with the keys in her left hand and something balled up in her right hand that he couldn't identify. He was so happy to see her and in such a hurry to get going that he didn't notice the dreamy look in her eyes until it was too late. She was right beside him handing him the keys when he saw her right hand swing up and realized what was in her hand. Before he could react, she pushed the Taser against the side of his neck and depressed the button, sending the high voltage shock through his body. The shock sent him crashing to the floor and before he could even begin to recover, Kayla stepped beside him and put her bare foot on his face.

"Great work lover." Kayla said to Laura, then she pulled up the robe she was wearing that she had found in Kayla's closet and lowered her ass down to his face-still twitching from the jolt. "You thought you were going to screw me over you piece of shit? I'll show you what I think of that. Open your fucking mouth."

Tom's head was still a bit clouded, so he did what she ordered. She leaned forward quickly and let loose with a steaming spray of sparkling urine which splashed up his neck and chin until it hit his open mouth. The shock snapped him out of his funk, and he snapped his mouth shut and twisted his head away, spitting out yellow fluid.

Kayla was not impressed and stopped her flow mid-stream. She grabbed both his ears and jerked his head back up then slid herself forward and planted her pussy right on his face. His broken nose was still very tender to the touch and when she plopped her weight down, he screamed in pain. Once again, she started peeing but this time it was right into his open mouth. She sat down hard which forced his mouth open wider and continued with her morning piss. She hadn't peed all night so there was a lot and Tom had no choice but to swallow the burning liquid or choke.

"Drink it you bitch!" she screamed at him as she relieved herself. She was looking into his wild eyes, watching his expression of fear and disgust turn into resignation and humiliation as he finished swallowing the rest of her golden stream. When she finally stopped, she raised up just a bit and had him lick her clean. Then she stood up and went to Laura. She leaned down and kissed her passionately on the lips, pushing her tongue deep into the other woman's mouth.

After a long lusty kiss Kayla stood up and went to her spray bottle. She proceeded to spray both her breasts, her pussy and her ass. She dropped the bottle then sexily strutted over to where Tom was still sitting on the couch. She put her left foot up on his chest and pushed him back until he was laying flat on his back again. Then she climbed up and straddled his face. Kneeling over his face she motioned Laura to join them.

Laura, even though she had spent the night getting her pussy buzzed with a powerful vibrator, was somehow still turned on and she crawled on top of Tom and stuck her face in Laura's swelling tits.

For the next thirty minutes, Kayla stayed kneeling over Tom's face letting him smell and lick her enhanced pussy scent while Laura rode his erection and breathed in the aroma from Kayla's breasts.

Chapter 15

Kayla's cell phone rang later that same day. It was early afternoon and she had applied the spray to herself every hour. She loved the way it made her feel, and she loved the way her clit was still growing longer. Her breasts and nipples were also getting larger too but to a lesser extent then her clit. She felt almost more than human, as if she was evolving into a super sexual woman. Her slaves (that's what she thought of them now) were more proof that she was better than everyone else.

So when her phone rang and the voice on the other end was Dr. Hewes and he was begging her to let him come see her, she was feeling more confident than ever. She had only gone to him yesterday and here it was less than twenty-four hours later, and he was already needing her. 'The spray is working faster' she thought, and she became even more excited. The thought that she could ensnare someone that soon was exhilarating. She checked the clock and told him that she would meet him at five o'clock and that he should bring her ten thousand dollars cash. She had already decided that she didn't ever want to go back to work again, and she knew that once people were addicted to her, they would do anything to get their next fix. She gave him Laura's address and told him not to be late.

Dr. Hewes didn't seem so happy with her telling him she wanted money, but he agreed to bring what she wanted. When she hung up, she was beaming from ear to ear with the thought of cashing in. She knew that all doctors made good money and that Dr. Hewes would be able to afford it.

Maybe the next person she enslaved would be a multi millionaire. Then she could get him to sign over everything to her and she would be set for life. She could travel the world in her own private jet and have her pick of any man or woman she wanted. Movie stars, famous athletes, recording artists, politicians, hell maybe a president or a king of some country even. She was sure that if she could get close enough, and with money that wouldn't be an issue, she could own anyone. All it would take is a few sprays of her special brew and then get close enough for them to smell it and that would be it. She would give them a taste, leave her number, then wait for them to call her. It was ingenious.

Get someone with enough money and she could buy her own lab and keep Laura around to make more of the special brew. She could live the high life and have everyone she wanted to be her slave.

She was confident that Laura was completely brainwashed after the events of the morning, and she was sure that Tom was almost there also. She figured that leaving Laura all night long with the panties over her nose had been enough to rewire her brain, otherwise she would have run with Tom that morning.

At five o'clock on the nose, the doorbell rang and when Kayla opened it, she was pleasantly surprised. Not only was Dr. Hewes standing there, but also his pretty secretary Miranda. She had nearly forgotten about Miranda.

Dressed in a thin robe and naked underneath Kayla welcomed them in "Well well, Dr. Hewes and Miranda, how nice. Please come in." she was acting like it was her house now and after a day of traipsing around naked it was certainly feeling like it was her house. She noticed the tell-tale signs of addiction from both doctor and secretary as they entered the house and she felt pride welling up inside her.

As they followed Kayla into the living room, they both gasped in unison as they came upon Tom who was tied naked to a wooden kitchen chair. His arms were behind his back and his legs were folded up and tied to the horizontal supports, so they weren't touching the floor. He also had a strip of duct tape pasted across his mouth and what they couldn't see was that he had Laura's soiled underwear from the previous night stuffed into his mouth.

"Oh don't worry about him,' Kayla reassured 'he was a very naughty boy earlier this morning so now he is in the time out chair." she walked over to him and pinched one of his nipples, twisting it painfully. She spun back around to face the two newcomers and said, "So Dr. Hewes, did you bring me what I asked for?"

The good doctor looked sick as he nodded his head and reached into the inside pocket of his suit jacket. He pulled out a thick envelope and held it up for Kayla to see. "I did, but I don't know why. You force this…this extremely addicting drug on us; for all we know it is extremely dangerous, and then you expect me to pay you to get more. How dare you do this to us. Just who the hell do you think you are?"

The whole time he was berating her, Kayla's bemused expression never wavered, but when he finished, she scowled and retorted "You had better watch yourself Dr. Dipshit. Piss me off and I won't give you what you came here to get. I can already see that your cravings are really bad, and they are only going to get worse. I can make your life hell, or I can give you what you came here for and you'll feel human again. The choice is yours. Either give me the cash or get the fuck out." She knew that this was hard for the good doctor and that made it so much more fun. Would he stay or would he go? She had a feeling that he would stay.

Miranda stepped forward and Kayla for the first time noticed just how miserable she looked. "Please, I don't have a lot of money and I can't pay you, but I need you, I need it so bad." She walked toward Kayla and just then, all hell broke loose.

The sound of glass shattering and the front door burst inward in an explosion of splinters, followed by several men rushing in wearing gas masks and carrying assault rifles. There was shouting men pointing weapons at everyone and ordering them all onto the floor. It was surreal, and in very short order, everyone was handcuffed in zip ties, their heads covered in black hoods, and they were led out to a line of waiting vans while the neighbors looked on in shock.

Chapter 16

Two men wearing biohazard suits led a blindfolded Kayla into a room that resembled a basement. She was brought over to a corner where her arms were locked into shackles that were hanging from the ceiling from a cable attached to a winch. One of the men pushed a button on the wall that activated the winch and lifted the shackles up until Kayla found herself up on her tiptoes.

"What the fuck are you doing to me?!?" She yelled into the blackness of the hood covering her face. "Please, just let me go and I won't call the police." She whimpered when she got no response.

Kayla was naked, having lost her thin robe at some time throughout the ordeal, and now she wondered what these people were going to do with her. As she hung there trying to free herself, she was hit with a blast of water from a garden hose. "AAAAUUUUGGGHHHH!!" she screamed as the cold water shocked her. It soon warmed up so that it was bearable, then the spray was directed away from her. She felt some cold liquid being squirted on her, then a soft scrub brush began to scrub her from head to toe.

The men were very thorough in scrubbing Kayla all over. The crack of her ass was even pulled apart and scrubbed clean. When they were satisfied that she was completely clean, her hood was finally removed, and the two men left the room, leaving Kayla crying and shivering.

When Kayla's eyes adjusted to the sudden brightness on the room, she looked around at the windowless room and concrete walls. There was a table with two chairs in the middle of the room and a water cooler in the opposite corner. Other than that, there was a hose attached to a spigot.

As Kayla hung shivering and dripping, the door opened and an attractive, bespectacled woman in a suit and leather skirt walked in. Her hair was done up in a bun and she carried a file and a pen in one hand and a folded towel in the other. She set the clipboard and pen on the table, then opened the towel.

"Who are you, and why am I here?" Kayla said through her chattering teeth. She was shivering badly now as the air in the room was cool.

"Hello Kayla. I'm so sorry that those barbarians treated you so badly." The woman said, bringing the towel over to Kayla. She began to wipe the water off. "I want you to know that you will not be hurt while you are here. The reason that you have been treated like this so far is because we had to take precautions. We didn't know where you had used the scent Kayla, and we couldn't afford to take any chances that someone would smell it. That is why you were completely washed down."

"So, you work for Scent Designs." Kayla said, "I should have known."

"I'm going to lower you down Kayla and unlock the shackles so we can sit down and discuss this. You should know that there are two armed guards right outside the door who will take you down if you try anything stupid though."

Kayla was lowered down and released from the shackles. She rubbed her wrists then wrapped the towel around herself before taking a seat.

"I've been hired to personally deal with your case Kayla." The woman said after she sat down opposite Kayla and opened the file that she had carried in. "My name is Helen Hansen, and I was given your file a few weeks ago. We know everything Kayla; about Arnold Peters, Tom Jensen, Laura Stanwick, Dr. Hewes and Miranda. You have been very busy these last few days Kayla."

"How do you know so much about me?" Kayla asked, feeling very vulnerable, and not just because she was naked.

"We've known about you since the very first time you promised Arnold Peters a blowjob if he got you stuff. Arnold may be desperate for love Kayla, but no one ever accused him of being disloyal to the company."

"That little prick." Kayla sneered under her breath.

"Well you would know about that now wouldn't you." Helen grinned a knowing grin, then tossed three pictures across the table to Kayla.

The top picture was obviously taken from a camera with a high-power zoom lens and showed Kayla and Arnold in the front seat of his car. She felt her stomach lurch as she realized that she been followed everywhere she went lately. She didn't want to look at the other two pictures, the memories of blowing that snivelling asshole were bad enough, but she thumbed the top one aside to see picture number two. In this one, Arnold's head was tilted back, his mouth opened in an 'O', and the back of Kayla's head could be seen over his crotch. The third picture showed Kayla sitting back up wiping her mouth with the back of her hand. She crumpled the three pictures in one hand and tossed them to the floor, looking angrily up at Helen.

"What do you want with me?" Kayla asked, grinding her teeth.

"Something had to happen Kayla. You have to realize that that we couldn't let you continue on the path you were taking. If you had just stayed with Tom, we would have watched you and him from afar. We would have studied you in your own environment. Unfortunately, you got greedy. You went from one person addicted to you to four people, in just a few days. You forced us to step in Kayla, and now we have to detox several people."

Kayla felt like a common addict who was in desperate need of a fix. Her body was craving her concoction and she was struggling to sit still and listen. Helen noticed her struggle.

"You need another fix don't you." It wasn't a question. "I can see you struggling right now."

Losing her cool, Kayla yelled "What the hell do you want from me?!?"

"We want to study you, Kayla. That's all. We want to allow you to continue using the scent to see what happens. We will have doctors here around the clock who will monitor your vitals and will put a stop to the experiment if your health deteriorates."

Kayla thought about it for a few moments before asking "And what if I refuse?"

"Well, in that case, we would have to call the cops Kayla. You have broken the law, and we have it all on film. And let's not forget how many people that you turned into addicts with just one sniff. Between the criminal and the civil cases Kayla, well you can imagine what kind of fun that will be. Of course, the choice is ultimately yours, and if you do decide to become our guinea pig, we would have you sign a contract, and pay you a salary."

Realizing that she not in any position to refuse, Kayla slowly nodded. She did like the idea of still being able to use the scent, but she didn't like the idea of not being able to control anyone. "I suppose that I don't have any choice in the matter." She said.

"Oh but you do Kayla. There are always choices, and if you choose to detox from the scent, jail is probably the best place to do that."

"I - I can't go to jail." She stammered. "I'll do whatever I have to do, just please, don't call the cops."

In reality, Helen never planned on calling the cops. That would mean far too many questions and the last thing that the company wanted or needed was the general public finding out about their experiments. The other people who had begun the testing of the scents had all signed a binding contract before testing had begun. After the problems with the product were obvious, the subjects were immediately put into detox and were all paid to keep quiet. They were also threatened with lawsuits if they told their story.

No, Helen never planned on calling the cops on Kayla. That was just a ploy to get Kayla to agree to what they planned on doing to her all along. She knew that Kayla would be needing another fix of the scent, and all they had to do was to leave her locked up in the cell for a few hours and she would be begging for more.

"Very well Kayla. I can tell you now that Tom and Laura have also agreed to sign contracts of their own. The good doctor and his secretary, since they were only exposed once, have been each given a shot of something to help them through their cravings. All traces should soon be out of their systems and they too will be paid for their troubles. You are making the right decision Kayla."

Three Months Later.

Kayla was lounging in her underwear across the room while watching Tom and Laura fucking. Laura was bent over the bed, her feet firmly on the floor with her legs spread wide and her head resting on the top of the mattress. Tom was standing behind her driving his cock into her pussy over and over again while she moaned.

"Does it feel good Laura? Do you like feeling Tom's fat cock in your hot, wet cunt?"

"Ohhh yeah unhhh yes, it fu - feels sooo good." she moaned.

"That's good. Just remember now that whoever cums first doesn't get to smell me again until tomorrow."

They had been fucking like this for several minutes, each had been holding out with all the willpower they could muster. Tom could sense that Laura was getting close to an orgasm, so he had picked up the speed and power of his thrusts, but that was also pushing him closer and closer to the point of no return. His body needed another hit of the special perfume and he couldn't bear the thought of waiting through the night to get it. He knew that Laura needed it as badly as he did, but he didn't care about that right now.

In an attempt to push Laura over the edge and make her start cumming first, Tom reached around to her breasts and started pinching her nipples. Her pussy clenched tightly around his shaft once and she moaned loudly, but somehow managed to hold off her orgasm.

Feeling that she would lose this challenge if she didn't do something right away, Laura reached one hand down between her legs, and as Tom drove his cock forward and his nutsack slapped into her engorged pussy, she grabbed his balls in her hand. Since he had been fucking her so vigorously and hadn't expected her to grab his balls, he wasn't able to stop until he had pulled more than halfway out and that caused his sack to be stretched and his balls were squeezed. It was just a tiny bit painful but being that he had been so close to cumming, this unexpected turn of events sent him past the point of no return, and with a cry of ecstasy and surprise, he began pumping his seed into Laura's pussy.

"OOOHHHHHSSSHHHIIITTTTT!!!" He screamed with a mixture of pleasure and anger. He was angry with Laura for tricking him like she had. He was angry with Kayla for coming up with this sick little game. But even more than that, he was angry with himself for losing control and cumming first, when he was so sure that he was going to win.

"Yes! He's cumming." Laura cheered. She had a good fuck and had won the competition meaning that she would be able to get what she so desperately wanted.

"Looks like you win this one Laura." Kayla said with a smile. She hooked her thumbs under the elastic band of her panties and pushed them down, her now giant clit, which had grown to seven inches long and as thick as a half dollar, sprung forth like a man's erect cock. "Come here now and claim your prize."

With a huge grin on her face, Laura pulled away from Tom and crawled across the room toward the massive appendage, putting her nose right up against the underside. Her tongue snaked out and licked around Kayla's fat pussy lips, while she breathed deeply of the scent that she craved.

Meanwhile, Kayla pinched her fat nipples which had grown to enormous size along with her breasts. Each nipple stood erect at over two inches in length while her breasts had ballooned to the size of basketballs. As she pinched the nipples, they both sprayed several pinhole sized streams of white milk.

Behind Laura, Tom had collapsed on the bed and was longingly staring at Kayla. He only wanted a sniff, just to set his mind at ease, and get him through the night.

"Tom, make yourself useful and clean Laura's pussy before it drips all over the floor." Kayla ordered, and Tom couldn't suppress a loud sigh and wrinkled brow, but he didn't bother to complain any more, as that would have likely led to him being put off even longer. Walking over on unsteady legs, Tom put his face into Laura's freshly fucked pussy, and began licking up the combined juices as they leaked from her steamy hole. The smell of sex was strong and musky and very erotic, but it was a far cry from what he needed from Kayla.

As part of the experiment, Kayla had been using an even greater amount of the scent than ever, and because of that, her body, when sexually stimulated, gave off the odor that Tom and Laura both craved. Being closer, Tom was able to smell traces of Kayla's addictive smell. It wasn't enough for him, but it was better than nothing.

Laura moved up to the tip of Kayla's clit/penis and sucked it deep into her mouth, swirling her tongue around the sensitive rod. Every breath she took filled her need as Kayla's entire body was giving off the scent now.

"OOOOOOHHHHHHHHH YYYYEEEEEAAAHHHH FFFFFFFFFFFFFFFFUUUUCCCCKKKK!!!" Kayla squealed in delight as her giant clitoris was sucked. Over the weeks and months that her clitoris had grown to the size of a cock, it had become more and more sensitive to even the slightest touch. But it wasn't just her clitoris that had grown either, her pussy lips swelled up also and her pussy was always wet with juices.

Laura swallowed almost all of Kayla's long clitoris, and at the same time, she slid two fingers past the extra puffy pussy lips into her throbbing cunt. Moans could be heard from both women as the smell of their juices filled the room.

On the other side of the wall stood three med techs, watching the proceedings through a large one-way mirror on the wall. The techs, two men and one woman, were all trying to keep things in perspective and stay in a scientific state of mind, recording and observing everything that happened next door. It was very difficult to be sure. The men were both trying to hide their erections, and the woman was secretly squeezing her legs together in an effort to put pressure on her vagina.

The room they were in was not much more than the size of a walk-in closet. It was connected to narrow halls that led to other tiny observation rooms, one for each room of the house that Tom, Kayla and Laura now shared.

The oldest of the three techs, a man named Blake, was the first to mention the heat. "Is it getting hot in here or is it just me?"

The woman in the group, a cute Chinese woman named Ling, was feeling the heat also and said, "I'll open a vent and let some air in.". The men in the room were so into the scene they were watching that neither one saw what vent she was opening, the one that led into the bedroom where the sex was taking place.

It took just a few minutes for the smell of the sex to reach all three techs, and without them even realizing it, they all slowly became addicted to Kayla's smell. As they all breathed in the fumes of addiction, their inhibitions were loosened, and they began to masturbate themselves openly. Within minutes, all three were tearing their clothes off and ten minutes later, when the next crew came in to relieve them, Ling was being sandwiched between her two colleagues, who were fucking her in the ass and pussy at the same time.

The whole room smelled heavily of sex and Kayla's special pheromones and as soon as the new crew came in, they too smelled it and became addicted. Shocked by what they were seeing in the observation room, they left the door open behind them, and Kayla's scent was sucked out into the rest of the building, infecting more and more people, each one quickly losing interest in stopping the spread. Before long, the powerful aphrodisiac scent had made its way throughout the building, carried through the air in the ventilation system to all corners and infecting every employee with lust for Kayla. World domination was just beginning.

www.ingramcontent.com/pod-product-compliance
Lightning Source LLC
Chambersburg PA
CBHW072123150726
47999CB00005B/2104